BOOK TWO
PARIS, 1850

BY SEBASTIAN ROOK

With special thanks to Ben Jeapes

SCHOLASTIC INC.
New York Toronto London Auckland Sydney
Mexico City New Delhi Hong Kong Buenos Aires

ISBN 0-439-63393-1

Series created by Working Partners Ltd.

Design by Steve Scott

12 11 10 9 8 7 6 5 4 6 7 8 9 10/0

Printed in the U.S.A.

First printing, September 2005

Chapter One

A small stone lay in Jack's way. He kicked it angrily and watched as it flew along the small, dank alley, skittering over the cobbles until it hit the wall and came to rest. Jack stalked moodily after it, his hands thrust into his pockets. He caught up with it, drew back his foot, and let the stone have it. "And *that's* for Master Benedict Cole," he growled as the stone shot away again.

Jack couldn't even remember what had brought him here. Some frustration lurked at the back of his memory. Something small, something trivial, but it was the tip of an iceberg of small and trivial somethings that had been building up in his new life with Ben and Emily and Mrs. Mills. *I probably held my knife and fork all wrong*, he thought bitterly.

It was early evening at the end of a warm day, and the breeze blowing down the alleyway carried scents that called to Jack's heart. He took a few more steps, turned a corner, and London's docks lay before him in all their glory.

"Ahhh . . ." he breathed. It was like coming home. He walked out onto the dockside and saw the ships huddled in their berths along the river. The familiar smell of sailcloth and damp ropes filled his nostrils, and he lost himself in the crowd of sailors and merchants, amid the hawkers and hustlers and hangers-on. Jack moved through the throng of people like a fish in a shoal.

"'Allo," he called cheerily to a group of lads who were loitering by a post. They looked at him dubiously, then pointedly turned their backs and carried on talking.

"Oh, all right," he muttered, feeling hurt. But then he glanced down at his clothes and saw himself through their eyes. His attire had been borrowed from Ben: gray woolen breeches, a jacket, and a baggy brown cloth cap. He had also put on a bit of weight since he'd moved in at Bedford Square, now that he was eating a daily diet of good food for the first time in twelve years. He looked like a young gentleman—not at all like the Jack Harkett who had lived here at the docks until a few months ago.

"Shouldn't have left," he muttered. "Shouldn't never have left." Five months of comfortable living in Bedford Square had almost made him forget all this, but now the memories came flooding back.

This, he realized as he looked around, was where it had all started. His footsteps had brought him to the dockside where the ghost ship had come in.

He sat down on a post, closed his eyes, and thought back. It had been early evening, like this, back in May. He had been sitting on this same post, eating a meat pie, and watching a ship come in.

He remembered the ship had been docking just as the

sun went down, and a cloud of bats had erupted from its hull and flown toward him. He had been so surprised that he had fallen off his perch. Jack's heart pounded at the memory.

The usual gang of dockworkers had hurried on board, but something terrible had scared them away. At that time, an intrigued Jack had been watching from behind a pile of crates. He glanced over to where the crates had been standing, but there was just a wall there now. So he turned back to where the ship had berthed, remembering the gentleman who had strolled easily down the gangplank and into the shadows. He had been followed by a boy of Jack's own age who had crept ashore, starving and frightened.

That boy had been Benedict Cole, and the tale he had told had held Jack spellbound in horrified fascination. Ben had stowed away on the ship in Mexico, the sole survivor of an expedition led by the eminent and respected biologist Sir Donald Finlay. Sir Donald had been Ben's friend—until he had become possessed by the Mayan vampire god, Camazotz, in the depths of the Mexican jungle. The bats on board the ship had been his vampire servants, and they had killed every man on the expedition, including Ben's father, Harrison Cole, and godfather, Edwin Sherwood. Then Camazotz, in the guise of Sir Donald, had brought them to England. And in the weeks that followed, Jack, Ben, and Ben's sister, Emily, had fought to destroy the vampire plague that threatened to consume London.

Jack was standing at the spot where Ben had first set foot on his return from Mexico. "Didn't know then, did I?"

he murmured to himself. He had left the docks only to escort his new friend home in the reasonable hope that there might be a reward in it for him. And there *had* been a reward, though not the one he had expected. He had been adopted into the Coles' home and treated as one of the family. He hadn't returned to the docks until now.

Jack's old instincts were coming back—perhaps they had never really gone. And one of those old instincts told Jack that he was being followed.

He moved casually to one side, then paused in the shadow of a pile of coiled chains. A moment later, a small boy crept slowly past, looking from left to right and wondering where his mark had gone. Jack grinned as he watched the kid. He was a bit younger than Jack, painfully thin, and raggedly dressed, with a dirty face and a bad haircut. For Jack, it was like looking into a mirror that showed an old reflection.

"Looking for me?" he called. The boy jumped, looking guilty. Jack tossed him a penny, which the boy caught without thinking. "See? Now you're better off than me."

The boy didn't ask what he meant, but scampered into the crowd. It was the safest thing to do, Jack knew, if you had been fingered. But he hadn't been joking. That penny had been his last. The little dock urchin was now richer than he was.

The sun had set and a full moon was rising over London. Jack looked around and fought back a shiver. He had learned to respect sunset because that was when the vampires came out to serve their master. Camazotz was gone now—at least he seemed to have left London—but other things came out at night, too. Dock dwellers who were tougher and harder than Jack had ever been. The kind of people who might see someone dressed like him and not take the time to inquire whether he actually *had* any money before roughing him up.

Jack quickly removed his jacket. That would serve to make him less conspicuous while he sought out some company—friends of his from the old days. He knew where he would find them.

He slung the jacket over his shoulder as he set off, and something heavy fell out of one of the pockets. Puzzled, Jack stared down at the dark ground where the object lay gleaming in the silvery moonlight. He bent down to retrieve it. "Oi," he said in genuine surprise. "Where did you come from?"

It was a small statue of a bat, solid and heavy in his hand. It reared up on its hind legs, wings outstretched and fangs bared. It glared at Jack through the dusk, its eyes full of hate.

Jack held it up, frowning in bewilderment. How on *earth* had it gotten into his pocket?

He knew exactly what it was. That summer, Sir Donald had stolen a valuable artifact from the British Museum—*this* artifact, to be precise. But Jack had only seen it a couple of times, and the last time it had been in the claws of Camazotz as he flew down through a crack in the earth to the fires of Hell.

The bat felt smooth and cold in his hand, and Jack remembered that it was made of pure gold. He hurriedly wrapped the statue in his coat, glancing around anxiously. Never mind the mystery, never mind how it got in his pocket—a wise man would not flash a gold statue around the docks.

Clearly Jack wasn't as poor as he had thought. But he still had no idea how he had come by the artifact. And he had more immediate worries—like the fact that he hadn't eaten since leaving Bedford Square, and that was a long time ago. The penny he had given the boy could have bought him some food. The priceless Mayan artifact he was now clutching would be harder to exchange for anything useful.

A snatch of laughter and the smell of cooking drifted toward him. He wasn't far from the Admiral Nelson now—the inn where he had taken the starving Ben Cole for his first decent meal in weeks. And they knew him there. He increased his pace, holding his coat and its precious cargo tightly.

The inn Jack remembered had grubby, whitewashed walls and a dark thatched roof. The only neat thing about it had been the sign over the doorway, which showed Nelson himself in his uniform. That board was washed and polished every day. As a boy, Bill, the landlord, had fought at Trafalgar under the great admiral. Nelson's name was respected like no other.

But now the inn had changed. Jack's eyes widened in surprise. It was still the same old building, but it was smartly turned out. The walls had been freshly painted and the thatched roof replaced with new tiles. Through the door he could hear the usual noises—laughter, shouting, and the tinkling notes of the off-key piano. But there wasn't the usual crowd hanging around outside. The place was *different*, and difference always made Jack suspicious. He had survived by understanding the way things were. Difference meant something new and unfamiliar.

Jack had always been tolerated at the Admiral Nelson, if not exactly welcomed by Bill. Jack could rarely pay for anything, which didn't help. The rule had always been that he was not to hang around the front, where he might put off the customers. But in his new clothes, Jack thought he could probably get away with it.

He approached cautiously, stooping slightly to peer through the door. The lights seemed dimmer than usual, but he could see into the front room. It was crowded with sailors and dock workers. Clouds of tobacco and wood smoke obscured his view of the bar.

Jack smiled to himself. He was being jumpy—perhaps because he had suddenly found the bat statue. So Bill had smartened up the place. So what?

Even so, for peace of mind, Jack followed a narrow alley around to the yard at the back. This was more like it. This was the side of the inn that he was used to. He had had many meals here. He leaned casually against the wall by the rubbish heap, so he had a clear view of the back door.

He didn't have to wait long. The light was soon blocked by the round, aproned figure of a woman carrying a bowl of scraps. She stopped dead when she saw Jack. "Jack! Jack

Harkett!" Molly put the bowl aside and, to Jack's surprise, ran forward. Before he knew it, she had pulled him into a tight hug. "So good to see you again, Jack! We thought you'd left us and gone off for good with that young gent you brought here!"

Jack, the breath squeezed out of him by Molly's strong arms, could only mumble in response. Molly had been like a mother to him. Her smuggled scraps had saved his life more than once. He was very fond of her, but he wasn't entirely comfortable with this show of affection.

She held him at arm's length to look at him. With surprise, Jack realized he was almost as tall as she.

"My, we's grown, hasn't we? You's put on a couple of pounds!" Molly declared. She prodded him in the stomach, making him squirm. "And dressed so smart, too."

Jack grinned. "Well, I'm back, ain't I?" He took the opportunity to look at her, too. Like the inn, she looked better than he remembered—younger and prettier. There was a rosy glow to her cheeks that had never been there before. He wondered if the inn was under new management. Maybe the new regime was doing her good.

As if reading his thoughts, she added, "Bill's still the same as ever, of course. Come in and see him."

Jack stared at her. "Really?"

"O' course, darlin'. He'll be glad to see you. Come on."

The back door led into the pantry, where a girl was scrubbing pots at the sink. Chopped vegetables and bloody scraps of raw meat were piled up on the rough wooden table, ready to be used in Bill's famous pies. Barrels of beer were stacked up against the far wall, next to the door that led into the front room.

Molly propelled Jack forward, with one hand at the small of his back. The next thing he knew, he was being pushed through to the bar.

The room fell silent. Jack flushed as everyone turned to stare at him. They didn't look overjoyed and they didn't look angry. They just *looked.* Jack swallowed and instinctively clutched his coat more tightly.

Molly came up behind him. "It's Jack!" she announced, and immediately the crowd cheered, then went back to its usual buzz as if he weren't there.

"Well, well." Bill had come around the bar. He was a large, bluff man with a gray beard. Jack blinked up at him. "Young Harkett, back where he belongs, eh?"

"Er, yes," Jack said. Something about all this didn't feel quite right. He wished he could put his finger on exactly what it was that was bothering him.

"Probably best, son." Bill patted him on the cheek. The gesture was so familiar and so unexpected that Jack recoiled. "Tell you what. T'show there's no hard feelings for"—he gazed at Molly with mock severity—"all them pies and whatnot, have a pint on the house."

Jack was shoved to the bar, and a wooden tankard was slammed down in front of him. Jack just looked at it. He was still grasping his coat and the bat statue it concealed in both arms. He didn't want to let go of it to take the beer.

"Shouldn't be doing this," Bill said, leaning forward with a smile that was somewhere between friendly and hateful, "knowing the company you keep. That young man you brought here? Nothing but trouble, he were."

Jack drew breath to defend his friend, but let it out again. He couldn't remember bringing Ben into the pub. In fact, he was sure Bill had never even met Ben. Something strange was going on, but he had no idea what. And the safest thing, he reckoned, was to pull out now.

"Look, I . . ." he began, starting to back toward the door. "I don't want to be no trouble. Thanks for the, um, pint . . . Bill . . . Molly . . . I'll be seeing you. . . ."

His eyes were fixed on the bar; he couldn't see what was behind him. The crowd must have been parting to let him through, though, because he hadn't walked into anyone.

Bill threw Jack a mocking salute, and then Jack felt himself bump into something. The crowd drew closer, their faces alight with expectation. And as Jack gazed at those faces, he realized that their eyes gleamed with an eerie red glow.

Strong hands grasped Jack's shoulders painfully from behind. He gasped and looked up into the eyes of a vampire. The fingers were tipped with sharp claws that curled around and pierced his sleeves. He felt them prick through his skin, and small flowers of blood welled up through the white cloth. The vampire growled and bent forward to drink his blood.

Jack felt the fangs sink into his throat, his flesh, his veins. . . .

Chapter Two

Ben Cole sat on the edge of Jack's bed, shaking him by the shoulders. "Jack!" he called. "*Jack!*"

Jack's eyes were tightly shut against the horrors that stalked his dreams, and Ben thought his shouts could probably be heard from the other side of Bedford Square. His screams had woken Ben in the next room. He had come straight through to find Jack in the grip of this terror.

Suddenly Jack went limp and opened his eyes.

"Are you awake?" Ben asked.

"I'm awake," Jack muttered.

Ben grinned. There was no mistaking that tone—the grumble of Jack afraid he had made a fool of himself. He gently released his friend, then sat back on the end of the bed.

Jack sat up and looked at his hands. Across each palm were four red gashes, just starting to ooze—he had clenched his fists so hard that his nails had drawn blood. "Guess it shows I'm still alive," he said in the same embarrassed tone.

Ben already knew what Jack's nightmare had been about. "I don't need to ask, do I?" Ben said quietly.

Jack shook his head. "It were vampires," he confirmed.

A tentative knock sounded at the door. "Jack?" called a voice through the wood.

Jack groaned. "Come in, Em," Ben called. Jack shot him a foul look. "Oh, sorry," Ben said, realizing belatedly that his friend might not want Emily to see him like this. But it was too late.

Ben's sister, Emily Cole, was already fully dressed, but her long auburn hair still tumbled loose down her back. She wore a long dark green dress over countless petticoats. She smiled at Jack and sat down on the other side of his bed.

Jack didn't meet her eyes. "Were I loud, then?" he asked.

"You were, rather," Emily agreed.

"The town crier knocked on the door and asked if you could keep the noise down," Ben joked. Jack looked up and gave Ben a reluctant smile.

"What was it about?" Emily asked.

Jack shrugged. "Hundreds of vampires down at the docks. They had me trapped," he replied.

Emily looked at him. "But they're all gone, Jack. We banished Camazotz for a thousand years, remember?" she said earnestly.

"Hmm," Jack murmured dubiously. "Try telling that to my dreams."

"If you like," Emily said with a smile. She rapped gently on Jack's head and leaned forward to call down one ear. "The vampires are gone!"

"Ha-ha," said Jack. He didn't find it funny.

"Jack," said Emily more seriously. "I know you're afraid that Camazotz might still be a threat, but you must remember the parchment Professor Adensnap showed us."

Jack listened sourly. He knew what was coming. Their friend Professor Adensnap had shown them an ancient parchment covered with Mayan writing. That writing had told them how to defeat Camazotz.

"It told us the blood rose would kill vampires," Emily continued. "And it did. It told us about the ritual. It told us about the potion. And it told us Camazotz would be banished. Everything else proved accurate, so we have to believe that bit, too. And besides, we *saw* him fly down into Hell," she added.

Jack sighed. "Yeah," he said glumly. Every word Emily said was true. But he couldn't forget what he had heard. He had been the last to leave the cellar where they had fought Camazotz. And just as he had been about to follow his friends out into the light, the voice of the demon god had echoed strangely inside his head, promising vengeance. That voice had made it very clear that Camazotz was *not* gone for good. He was lurking somewhere—watching and waiting—and he was *very* angry.

But, Jack sometimes wondered, had he *really* heard the

voice of Camazotz? It had been months since the battle, and he had seen no sign of a vampire. Indeed, the vampire plague in London had cleared up overnight.

Perhaps Emily was right. Perhaps there was nothing to fear from the vampire god anymore. Even though he wanted to, Jack simply didn't believe that was true.

He sighed—and was saved from having to reply by a sharp rap on the door.

"Master Jack!" called a voice.

Jack groaned again. "Piccadilly bloomin' Circus!" he said. A moment later, Mrs. Mills opened the door and swept in. "Getting crowded in here," Jack muttered under his breath.

The widowed Mrs. Mills had been housekeeper to the Coles since before Emily and Ben could remember. She was short and portly and usually wore gray or black. She could be fierce, but Ben knew it was only because she loved him and Emily more than she would ever say. She even appeared to be quite fond of Jack. Emily and Ben had pressed her to let him stay with them after they had defeated Camazotz, but Ben knew she wouldn't have allowed it if she hadn't already taken a liking to their friend.

However, sometimes you had to look very hard to find that liking. "Really, Master Jack, such a racket!" she scolded. "And look at you now." She bustled over and felt his forehead, then ran her fingers through his thick brown hair. It was still damp with sweat after his nightmare. "You need a bath. Tillet will run one for you now. And you, Master

Benedict—back to your room and get dressed. Come on, come on . . . oh!"

Jack had been surreptitiously wiping his stinging palms on the sheet, and he had left a bloodstain. Mrs. Mills spotted it at once. She grabbed his palm and turned it toward her. Then she took his other hand, more gently, and studied that, too. "Well . . ." Her tone was suddenly softer. "Well, Master Jack, if you would trim your nails more diligently, perhaps this would not have happened. Take your bath, and then I'll put something on these scratches for you. Now, Master Benedict, Miss Emily, out!"

Jack had fought vampires. He had fled from them with his friends through the dark maze of Soho. He had done battle with them in their stronghold and he had even faced down their master, the Mayan demon god Camazotz. So he thought he could handle toast.

Jack looked at Emily, who was sitting across from him at the breakfast table in the dining room of the Coles' house in Bedford Square. It should be so easy. He had thought you would just take a slice, take a knife, slap on whatever you wanted, and then eat it. Then he had seen Emily buttering her own toast. She held the butter knife daintily between two fingers. She took a thin sliver of butter, barely enough to cover the slice, and applied it. Jack presumed this was how it was done by people who lived in Bedford Square.

Now that he lived in Bedford Square, too, perhaps he should learn to do it their way.

He took his own butter knife, trying to imitate Emily. You pressed it onto the toast, just *so*. . . . The slice snapped in two and Jack dropped his knife with a clatter. He looked up, his face blazing red.

"Don't eat like a girl, Jack," Ben said casually. He was fully dressed now, with his fair hair neatly brushed, and he sat at the head of the table, in his father's place, reading the newspaper. He smeared a slice of his own toast with large quantities of butter and marmalade, then took a massive bite.

"Oh, Ben, honestly," said Emily. Ben looked up from the paper and gave Jack a wink. Jack grinned back.

Mrs. Mills opened the door. "The mail has arrived, Master Benedict," she said. "There are some items I would like you to look at with me, after you've eaten."

"Right you are, Mrs. Mills," Ben said, with no great enthusiasm.

It had been hard, after Camazotz had been banished, to tell Mrs. Mills the truth about her employer, Harrison Cole. But Ben and Emily had had to inform her that their father was dead. In his will, Harrison had nominated their godfather, Edwin Sherwood, to become their legal guardian. Unfortunately he was presumed dead as well. Harrison's will had stipulated that, in the event of Edwin Sherwood's death or absence, Mrs. Mills was to continue looking after

Ben and Emily. Since their mother's death, Mrs. Mills had become a very dear and trusted member of the household, and now, together with the family lawyer, she looked after Harrison's considerable estate.

When Emily turned twenty-one—in another eight years—she would inherit a large set of funds. But Ben was the boy, and although he was a year younger than his sister, when he reached twenty-one he would inherit the estate itself. Mrs. Mills intended that by then he should be fully trained in the running of it. She took pains to show Ben the bills and the accounts so that he knew exactly how his father's money was being handled. It was hardly Ben's favorite activity but was a bit like learning Latin—tedious and not immediately useful, but one day, who knew?

The doorbell rang. "I wonder who that could be?" Mrs. Mills said, and disappeared to answer the door.

The three friends heard the door open and a man's voice say, "Well, good morning, dear lady!"

"Why, Professor Adensnap," Mrs. Mills replied. "What a pleasant surprise. Do come in. The young people are still at breakfast, but you may certainly wait in the drawing room. The curtains have been drawn back."

"Dear lady, you would light up any room, curtains or none," declared the professor gallantly as he walked down the hallway. They heard Mrs. Mills smother a girlish giggle.

Jack put his head in his hands. Ben and Emily rolled their eyes at each other.

Mrs. Mills came back in to announce that their friend Professor Adensnap would like to see them when they had finished eating.

The drawing room was lit by a large, south-facing window that looked out onto Bedford Square. Like many other rooms in the house, one wall was lined with books—the legacy of Harrison Cole's career. A softer, more homey touch came from the light yellow wallpaper and the warm golden color of the sofa and chairs. It was a tranquil room, full of pale October light. The professor was browsing through a book when Emily, Jack, and Ben came in, followed by Mrs. Mills.

"My dear young friends!" The professor's spectacles slid down his nose as he looked at his friends. His clothes had once been smart, though now they were a little shabby and out of date. He had the money to buy new ones but little inclination to waste time on fashion. His voice sounded weak, but they all knew the strength and wisdom of the old professor. He looked at them out of clear blue eyes and ran one hand over his rumpled white hair. "You are looking well," he remarked. "How are your studies progressing?"

The question meant different things to each of them. Emily was determined to carry on her father's work in deciphering the ancient Mayan language and understanding their once great civilization. Ben, on the other hand, had surprised everyone by turning to biology. He had enjoyed looking after the living zoological specimens during the Mexico expedition and, as he put it, studying dead things had killed their father. Studying life was more rewarding. Neither Jack nor Emily had pointed out to him that Sir Donald Finlay had also been a biologist—and he had ended up possessed by Camazotz.

For Jack, "studies" meant simply reading and writing. Like many of London's street children, he'd had no education—until he'd met Ben and Emily. Now he could read and write the whole alphabet, and he was beginning to tackle simple sentences.

They all began to answer at once, but Adensnap was barely listening. "Splendid, splendid," he said. "Dear friends, I have a proposal. A suggestion. A treat! I've had an invitation from m'good colleague Henri, the vicomte de Montargis."

"What's a vicomte?" Jack whispered to Ben.

"Same as a viscount," Ben replied.

There was a brief pause. Then—"What's a viscount?" Jack asked.

"A kind of lord," Ben told him quietly.

"Montargis . . ." Emily was saying thoughtfully. "Why, of course! He was a student of Dampierre—the French archaeologist who was an expert on the New World. The Vicomte de Montargis took over when Dampierre died. He's the greatest French authority on the ancient American civilizations."

"Precisely, dear girl," said the professor. "And he has invited me to speak at a symposium on Mayan culture at the Louvre Museum in Paris. It is being held next week. Mrs. Mills permitting, I propose to take all three of you with me. I'm sure it will be a valuable addition to your education."

"Blow my education!" Jack said, but only to himself. The professor wanted to take him to Paris, to meet a kind of lord! That was all the reason he needed for going.

Three shining faces turned to Mrs. Mills.

"Of course you may all go," she said, laughing. "But naturally, I will expect you to continue your studies on the journey."

Jack barely heard her. *Paris!* he thought excitedly. He had whiled away many a day at the docks dreaming of traveling. He had imagined taking passage on one of the hundreds of ships crowding the port of London and sailing off to faraway lands. Such daydreams had led to Jack's meeting Ben and everything else that had followed. But so far, the farthest he had actually traveled was to Kew Gardens—all of ten miles away. He had never even seen the sea.

"I'm sure you have plans to make, Professor," said Mrs. Mills. "I'll leave you and your young friends to it."

She smiled as she closed the door behind her. The professor bowed, then immediately straightened up. He leaned forward as if he was about to share a great secret.

"There is one other thing," he said. His eyes twinkled

with excitement. "Henri has the eye artifact that Dampierre discovered. I thought you would like to see it."

News of the trip to Paris had temporarily driven all thought of vampires from Jack's head, and the professor's words were an unwelcome reminder. Jack had heard of the eye from his friends. It had been discovered in South America and brought back to France by Dampierre. What made it particularly significant with regard to vampires was the fact that it had probably been made by the same craftsman who created Camazotz's golden bat—the same golden bat that Camazotz had stolen from the British Museum and that had haunted Jack's recent nightmare.

The friends had never discovered why the golden bat statue was of such importance to Camazotz. But it seemed to Jack that if the vampire god was interested in the bat, he might be interested in the eye, too. Jack decided grimly that he should probably make the most of this chance to see the eye. If Camazotz's last words proved to be more than an empty threat—or the product of his own overwrought imagination—then the more he could learn about the vampire god, the better.

The professor was still talking. He had proudly produced a newspaper from his bag. "Look," he said. He shook it out so they could see the front page. "Henri sent me this copy of the *Gazette des Tribunaux*. The symposium made the front page!"

" 'The Vicomte de Montargis has announced he is to chair a symposium on the lost civilization of the Mayan people,'" Emily read aloud. She spoke slowly, translating from the French as she went. Ben read over her shoulder.

Jack just glanced at the article out of polite interest. He could barely read English, let alone French. He let his eyes roam over the page. He decided to practice his reading skills on the next-largest headline. One word caught his eye. "*Londres*," he said. "Ain't that French for London?"

"Yes," replied Ben. "Why? Oh." He followed Jack's gaze and quickly scanned the text. "It's nothing, Jack. Something about an illness . . . er . . . faintness, loss of strength . . . contagious anemia similar to the recent wave of illness in London. . . . Don't worry, Jack, it seems that Paris has just as many illnesses going around as London does. Go on, Emily."

"'Eminent and enlightened thinkers from all over Europe will descend upon the capital,'" Emily read.

Jack sank down into an armchair, deep in thought. The only recent wave of illness in London to fit the description in the Paris newspaper was Camazotz's vampire plague. A few months earlier, the London papers had been full of reports that people from all over the city, rich and poor alike, were dying of sudden, inexplicable blood loss. Only Ben, Jack, and Emily had realized that it was because Camazotz was recruiting and feeding his army of vampires. When the friends had finally managed to banish Camazotz and his vampire servants, life had returned to normal. And London, a city well used to spates of cholera and typhoid, had soon forgotten about the outbreak.

But if the French were now suffering from the vampire plague, then Camazotz must be in Paris. Jack looked with resignation at his friends, who were still immersed in news of the symposium. They firmly believed that Camazotz was safely banished for a thousand years. But the newspaper story had confirmed Jack's worst fears. Another confrontation with the vampire god loomed on the horizon, he was sure.

Jack now looked forward to the Paris trip with a grim determination. He prayed that he was wrong and that this adventure would prove a little *less* exciting than the last.

Chapter Three

"Come *on*, Jack!" Ben's impatient call came up the stairs. It was a rainy October morning, three days after the professor had come to visit. Ben, Emily, and their bags were waiting on the pavement outside the house. Jack had mumbled a quick excuse and run up to his room.

He pulled open the drawer of his dresser and took out a small tin. He looked at it thoughtfully, then checked the contents—a carefully preserved stem of blood rose—and slipped the tin into his pocket. He turned to the door. "Coming!"

A few minutes later, the professor turned up, commanding a four-wheeler carriage. A hansom cab followed. The friends piled their bags into the hansom, then climbed into the four-wheeler. They bade good-bye to Mrs. Mills and were off to Paris.

A rattling train journey soon brought them to the great port of Dover. The ferry waiting at the docks had two great wheels and a tall, thin funnel jutting out of the deck. For a moment Jack hesitated at the bottom of the gang-plank. After all his years of living on the docks, he was about to take his first journey by boat. The others casually walked on board ahead of him. Jack patted his pocket to check that the tin was still there, then followed.

Stewards showed the passengers down a flight of steps to the promenade deck, an enclosed area at the stern. It was such a short crossing—two and a half hours—that the professor hadn't booked them a cabin. Passengers had to jostle for the wooden benches that lined the deck. Jack pressed through the crowd with muttered "'scuse me's" and "mind out's" and got them all a seat on the stern bench. It was right by the great window that stretched from one side of the boat to the other.

"Thank you, dear boy," the professor said gratefully when he, Emily, and Ben had finally caught up. They settled down next to Jack, hugging their bags.

Jack twisted around to peer out the window. "I'm going to watch us leave!" he said, jumping to his feet.

He was up on the main deck, looking out across the channel, when the ship's whistle blew and steam billowed up out of its funnel. He saw the mighty wheels creak into action and the paddles lowered into the water. The wheels spun and the paddles dug in, beating the water into foam. The ship shuddered as it moved away from the dock.

Jack stood at the stern rail and watched as the town and cliffs of Dover receded. Then he shivered. A cold wind was blowing down the English Channel. He turned away, staggering slightly. The deck was shifting beneath his feet and he did not enjoy it. He made his way carefully to the top of the steps and looked down on the warmth and light of the promenade deck. Cautiously he put a foot forward, then another. No, he really did not like what was happening to him.

The oily smell of the engines, mixed with the stale, dead stink of the bilgewater, drifted up out of the hatchway.

Jack's insides heaved. He fled to the side of the ship and vomited into the sea. And that was how he spent the rest of the voyage.

Chapter Four

"It's not your fault, dear boy," said the professor cheerfully. They were shuffling down the gangplank at the Calais docks. "Plenty of chaps, young and old, get seasick."

Finally they set foot on the soil of France. Jack couldn't care less that it was another country. It just mattered that it stayed still.

They followed the crowd into Customs. Officials in small round caps and black uniforms stood at the tables, inspecting everyone's bags.

As Jack had his luggage inspected, the man glanced at him. "*Ça va pas?*" he said cheerfully. *You are ill?*

"*Oui,*" Jack muttered. "*J'ai le mal de mer.*" *Yes. I am seasick.* He didn't notice that Ben and Emily were staring at him as if he had grown another head.

The official smiled and glanced from side to side, making a game of being a conspirator. He plucked a crumpled paper bag from his coat and held it out. "*Tiens—manges ce gingembre. Tu iras mieux!*" he said. *Have some ginger. You'll feel better.*

Jack peered into the bag. It was full of lumps of

crystallized ginger. He warily took one and popped it into his mouth. "*Merci!*"

"I didn't know you could speak French!" Ben exclaimed as they left the shed.

Jack beamed. The ginger was already settling his stomach, and the surprise he had given his friends made him feel even better. "Well, enough to get some ginger," he said cheekily. "Why? Can't you?"

"Of course I can —" Ben began irritably.

"He's teasing, Ben." Emily laughed.

"Still, an unexpected accomplishment, young Jack," remarked Adensnap with a smile.

"Lots of French sailors at the docks," Jack told him. "You soon picks it up. O' course I don't speak it as fancy as you." He looked up at the signs above their heads. As with English, he could only *speak* the language, not read it. "Where do we go now?" he asked.

"The train's this way," the professor replied, taking the lead.

By now it was almost eight o'clock in the evening. The next train to Paris wasn't for some time, so they made their way to the waiting room. Professor Adensnap seemed to have much more energy than his age would suggest. He was still wide awake and content to read a book. The others were tired from their early start and the long journey, and in the warmth of the waiting room their eyes grew heavy. Ben and Emily huddled together and tried to sleep for an hour, wrapped snugly in their coats. Other passengers around them were doing likewise, though the plain wooden benches made it difficult. Jack had slept on worse. He wedged himself into a corner of the room, checked the tin in his pocket one more time, then closed his eyes.

Fangs sank into his throat, his flesh, his veins. . . .

Jack gasped and opened his eyes. For a moment, he wasn't sure what was real and what was just a dream. What he *did* know was that something was wrong. His instincts told him it was so—instincts that had never failed him in all his years of eking out a living at the docks.

He looked around, desperately trying to pinpoint what had disturbed him. He was surrounded by dozing passengers. Ben and Emily were asleep, and the professor . . .

The professor was slumped in his seat and his book had slipped to the floor. A tall man in a long black cloak was bending over him. It was a sight Jack had seen in a hundred nightmares.

"Vampire!" Jack howled, and flung himself at the man.

Chapter Five

Ben was woken by Jack's shout. He opened his eyes just in time to see his friend hurl himself at a stranger in a black cloak. Jack's head cannoned into the man's midriff and his weight threw the man to the floor. Jack sat firmly on top of him. With one hand he was scrabbling at something in his pocket. Still half awake, Ben dimly noticed him pull a small tin from his coat and wrench it open. He took something from inside and slashed at the man with it. The stranger shouted angrily and grabbed Jack's hand.

"No!" Jack was yelling fiercely. "You won't get the professor! I got blood rose to deal with the likes of you. Ben, wake up!"

"*Laissez moi!*" the man shouted. *Let me go!* Ben could see there was a nasty red scratch down the side of his face.

Now everyone in the waiting room was awake. Ben knelt down next to Jack and patted him on the back. "Jack," he said mildly, "what are you doing?"

Jack turned his head to stare at his friend. Ben could see that even though his eyes were wide open, he was still only half awake.

"I got blood rose, he's a vampire. . . ." Jack panted.

To his surprise, Ben saw that Jack was holding a small sprig of blood rose. It was only a few inches long but the thorns were unmistakable. The friends had found the blood rose in the botanical gardens at Kew. It had been their first and best weapon against the vampires before they had banished Camazotz. He had had no idea that Jack had saved any of it.

"I don't think he is, Jack," he said firmly. Jack looked down at his victim and shook his head. Ben could see the confused wakefulness dawning on his face. One scratch from a blood rose was fatal to a vampire. If this man had belonged to Camazotz, he would be a pile of ash by now.

"But . . . the prof . . . he was just lying there," Jack began.

"Why, goodness me," said Adensnap, sitting up and pushing his glasses back into place. "I must have dropped off." He picked up his book and smoothed out the pages.

Emily helped Jack to his feet. "Don't worry, there really aren't any more vampires," she reassured him quietly. "And I think you should let this gentleman go now."

Ben stood up and helped the man to his feet. The stranger shot Jack an angry glare, which Jack returned with a scowl.

"He were bending over the prof," Jack grumbled. "Looked like he were going to bite him."

The man swore in French. Ben and Emily tried to apologize, but he dismissed them with an angry gesture. But as he turned to go, he was suddenly brought up short. The handle of Adensnap's umbrella was snagged in his belt, while the other end was held firmly in the professor's grasp.

"Of course, as our new friend is completely innocent and human," said the professor, "he won't object to opening up his coat for our inspection? Just in case something *accidentally* fell into his pocket, you understand?"

The man swore again and knocked the umbrella aside, but Ben understood what the professor was getting at. He moved quickly to stand between the man and the door. Jack, now fully awake, joined him. Together the boys had faced Camazotz. A simple pickpocket didn't frighten them.

For a moment the man looked as if he might run, but then he seemed to change his mind. "I think . . . you drop . . . this?" he said in hesitant English as he reached into his pocket and produced the professor's leather wallet.

Adensnap's eyes twinkled. "Why, how gracious. Yes, I believe that *is* mine," he replied, holding out his hand.

The waiting room was suddenly a flurry of passengers patting their pockets and checking their bags. The man took the opportunity to drop the wallet and disappear quickly through the doors.

"Should we go after him, Professor?" asked Ben. "Take him to the police—the gendarmes?"

Adensnap smiled. "Dear boy, I have said it before—let everyone play to their strengths. We four do a very nice job at battling demon gods. Let us not hog the limelight, eh? We'll leave the thief-catching to those whose job it is."

"Where did the blood rose come from, Jack?" asked Emily as they sat back down on one of the wooden benches.

Jack shrugged. "I kept some. Thought it might come in handy." He looked wistfully at the little branch—barely more than a twig—that he was still holding.

"I don't think it will be handy for much longer," Ben said frankly. "It looks half dead."

And Jack had to admit that it did look pretty far gone. Perhaps he should have looked after it more carefully. After all, flowers kept in tins weren't known to thrive. He rubbed it with his fingers, and the twig snapped. It was dry and brittle. He threw it to the floor with a sigh.

"And Camazotz —" began Emily.

"I know, I know. Camazotz is gone," Jack interrupted. Then he sighed deeply. "Maybe you're right."

Ben gave him a friendly nudge. "Cheer up, you're allowed to be pleased about it, you know."

Jack gave his friends a tired smile as a piercing whistle from outside announced that their train had arrived.

It was fortunate that the train was comfortable, because it was delayed at Amiens and didn't arrive in Paris until midmorning. The friends disembarked and fought their way through the crowds and crates of produce stacked on the platform. Jack was smiling to himself as he looked around—he was in a foreign city at long last. The hustle and bustle reminded him of London.

Then he frowned, because he had seen something else that reminded him of London: A middle-aged man, gaunt and very pale, staggered to the wall and had to lean against the stonework for a moment. He looked as if he had barely enough strength to stay on his feet.

Jack remembered seeing men like that in London as the vampire plague had begun to take over the city. But he shook his head to drive away the memory, and when he looked again, the man had already been swallowed up by the crowd. Jack decided he wasn't going to make the same mistake he'd made in the waiting room twice. Camazotz, he told himself firmly, was *gone*.

Chapter Six

The professor flagged down a coach and gave directions to the driver. A porter loaded their bags onto the back of the carriage, and they were off. Ben and Adensnap sat facing Emily and Jack, who had his face pressed to the window. The carriage lurched into a particularly large pothole and Jack hit his forehead on the glass. He rubbed his head ruefully and gave the road a dirty look. Then he gazed out at Paris again.

Emily smiled to herself and looked out the window on her own side. Even on a dull October day, Paris was full of light. The open streets, the parks, and the low buildings let the sun reach the ground. And even though the roads were in worse condition than London's streets, the architecture was generally more ornate and intricate than anything in England's capital. Paris was a beautiful city.

Their hotel was on the Rue de Rivoli, opposite the Louvre Museum. They checked their bags in, then hurried across to the gallery so that the professor could introduce them to his friend the Vicomte de Montargis.

The Louvre, a former palace, was an imposing building

of grand arches and pillars. The core of the museum was a square fortress around a large courtyard. Adensnap led the friends through the great main entrance and along the Grande Galerie. Archways opened up on either side. Long corridors packed with art treasures from all over the world stretched away as far as the eye could see.

They found the South American gallery on the top floor. It was long and wide, with polished flooring, full of daylight from skylights in the ceiling above. Emily's eyes lit up at the sight of the first exhibit, a stone head carved into a square pillar. It was unmistakably Mayan or Aztec. The eyes were square, carved on either side of a square nose and above a wide, grinning rectangular mouth with square stone teeth.

"Aha!" said the professor, beaming. "Our friend Chac. Do you remember him?"

All three friends nodded. When they first met Professor Adensnap, he had told them about some of the Mayan legends. Emily remembered that Chac, lightning god of the Maya, had been the archenemy of Camazotz. His followers had led the rebellion against the vampire god, and his priests had invented the ritual that had banished Camazotz for a thousand years.

"He doesn't look very friendly," Emily said.

"Oh, he wasn't *friendly*, dear girl," remarked Adensnap. "None of the Mayan gods were. But he was the enemy of Camazotz. He taught the Maya how to grow vegetables and he protected their cornfields. So he can't have been completely bad. Well, come on through." He led them to an archway that opened into a narrow passage lined with many doors. He knocked on the door at the far end.

A man's voice called through the wood, "*Qui va?*"

"Adensnap," answered the professor. There came a muffled exclamation through the solid wooden paneling and the sound of hurrying footsteps, then the door was hauled open.

"*Mon cher Alfred!*" cried an elegant man whom Emily took to be the Vicomte de Montargis.

"Henri!" replied the professor with a smile.

The vicomte was tall and well built, dwarfing the professor. He had crisply trimmed silver hair and a short, neat beard. He wore a well-tailored gray morning suit with tails. His dark eyes were hidden behind a gold pince-nez that, unlike Adensnap's spectacles, always stayed on. The vicomte pulled Adensnap into a huge hug and kissed him on both cheeks.

Jack's eyes grew wide with horror. "He kissed him!" he whispered. Ben and Emily both nudged him to keep quiet.

"Alfred, my dear fellow, it is so good to see you again, and . . ." The vicomte finally became aware that Adensnap wasn't on his own. He cocked an eyebrow at the three friends, who were waiting patiently behind the professor. "You have brought company? I did not believe you were a family man."

"Oh! My manners!" Adensnap laughed. "May I present Miss Emily Cole, Master Benedict Cole—the children of Harrison Cole, you know—and Master Jack Harkett. All three have been invaluable to me in my, um, researches."

"Ah!" The vicomte's face lit up. He bowed, took Emily's hand, and kissed it solemnly. "Montargis at your service, mademoiselle," he said. He straightened up and looked at the boys. Emily saw Jack brace himself; she presumed it was in case the vicomte tried to kiss him, too. But the Frenchman simply said hello to both of them, then turned back to Adensnap. "Children . . ." he said thoughtfully.

Adensnap's face fell. "I hope I did not take too much for granted in bringing them, Henri? They are possessed of very keen minds."

"Eh? Oh, no. *Au contraire.*" The vicomte smiled broadly. "You have no idea what a service your young friends could provide. Pray, come in, my dear fellows."

A service? A flush of pleasure ran through Emily at the thought that she could be of service to the great Montargis! What could he possibly want of her? She hurried forward as he ushered them into his office.

The room was wide and spacious. It had a large bay window from floor to ceiling, with a balcony outside. Beyond that they could see the river Seine. The walls were lined with bookshelves, only broken where a door led through into the adjoining office. Emily ran her gaze eagerly over the collection—so much knowledge, so much to learn. . . .

"*Mon oncle? Que se passe-t-il?*"

Emily jumped. A girl sat in a chair by the window, kicking her heels against its wooden legs. She looked about

Emily's age—thirteen. Her hair was dark and curled in ringlets over her shoulders. Around her neck she wore a small, square stone pendant. She stood up as they came into the room. She looked sulky as she said, "*Mon oncle* —"

"Dominique, these are guests from England—Emily, Benedict, Jack, and Professor Adensnap. You speak English as well as I do, so let us show them some courtesy," the vicomte interrupted.

The girl pouted at the friends, looking at them unenthusiastically, as if, Emily thought, they were last season's fashions. "Welcome to Paris," Dominique said sullenly. Her French accent was strong, but her English was easy to understand.

"Dominique is my niece from Toulon. She's staying with me while her mother recuperates," said the vicomte. He lowered his voice to speak directly to Adensnap. "And you would do me *such* a favor if your young friends were to take her off my hands for an hour or two." There was a note of desperation in his tone.

"We —" Ben began, then bit his lip. He exchanged a glance with Emily. She could guess what he was thinking, because her thoughts were the same. *We come all the way from England for a symposium on Mayan civilization and you want us to nursemaid your bored niece!*

"I have just the thing!" the vicomte said suddenly. "You shall take —"

"Oh, Uncle, no, not the special tour!" Dominique protested. "I have been on the special tour so many times."

"Then you may help the guide with your additional knowledge," the vicomte said firmly. He pulled the door open and bellowed, "Gaston!"

A young man in his early twenties appeared a moment later.

"Gaston, these are my friends from England. They have some empty hours to fill. Give them the tour. The *full* tour." He winked at the three friends. "This is something I have always wanted to do myself, but I can never find the time. You can tell me all about it afterward. Now, Alfred and I have so much to discuss, so, until later!"

And before they knew quite what had happened, the three friends and Dominique found themselves standing with Gaston on the other side of the door as it shut behind them.

Chapter Seven

Gaston looked gloomily down at them. "Come," he said glumly, and turned away. They trooped silently after him.

"You probably know the Louvre was once a palace," Gaston said in excellent English. "The history of this wing in particular . . ."

Jack could feel the boredom settling in already. He looked casually around for some distraction. There were other visitors about, drifting from one display to another. Jack smiled to himself. There had been a time when he would have been sizing up the crowd. Which were the couples? They were always good targets because a man didn't want to appear harsh and unkind in front of his lady. Who was on their own? Ladies could often be nice and sympathetic, ready to hand over a penny for an errand. Failing that, which men looked as if they would never miss a note or two from the fat wallets in their pockets?

And then Jack's smile turned into a broad grin. There was a boy on the other side of the gallery, younger and smaller than he. The lad wasn't finely dressed. The collection of patches that adorned his rough cloth coat and trousers said that he and Jack would have once had a great deal in common. He walked casually along a display of small stone carvings, trailing his fingers over the items. *Any moment now*, Jack thought, *one of those carvings is going to mysteriously disappear. . . .*

"You!" A museum attendant, an elderly man with a massive mustache, had suddenly noticed the ragamuffin. The man ran at the boy, waving his hands, and the boy fled with a cheeky grin on his face.

He ran straight through the small group of Jack, Ben, Emily, Dominique, and Gaston. Gaston glared after him and muttered something in French.

Good luck! Jack thought, with a last look at the boy's receding back.

"Now, please come this way," said Gaston, and Jack had to return his attention to the tour.

Despite his misgivings, what followed was actually interesting. Gaston was an assistant curator and he had made the history of the building an area of expertise. "The museum dates from 1793 as the Musée de la République," he said as they walked down a dim spiral staircase. They were surrounded by ancient stone and the only light came from the oil lamp in Gaston's hand. They were already in a part of the museum that the public didn't usually see. "But the building itself dates from 1200."

"Philippe Auguste began by building a fortress on the north bank of the Seine," said Dominique, sounding bored, "but the Louvre as we see it today wasn't finished until—"

"Until the reign of Henri the Fourth," Gaston interrupted, in a vain attempt to regain control of the tour.

"He was Henri the Third of Navarre," put in Dominique. "But when Henri the Third of *France* was assassinated, he became Henri the Fourth of France, too."

"Do the French still chop people's heads off?" Jack murmured to Ben.

"From time to time," Ben whispered back.

"Not as often as they should, if you ask me!" Jack muttered, glancing at Dominique. Ben grinned and punched him on the arm. Emily glared at them both, and the boys bit their lips and tried to look sorry.

Gaston took the little group down to the deepest basements of the building. They walked along the medieval moat under the Cour Carrée, where they could reach out and touch the ancient stones of the original fortress. They saw the dungeons where many had come to a nasty end. And then Gaston took them up through the many levels of the palace to the sculpture gallery.

"The *Venus de Milo,*" Gaston announced proudly. "She was discovered in the second century before Christ on the island of Milos, and Louis the Eighteenth bought her for six thousand francs in 1820."

Standing six feet tall, the body of the white marble statue was curved and elegant. She stood with her weight on one foot, and her blank eyes gazed at a point off to one side.

Jack stared—for several reasons. For a start, he wasn't used to seeing women with their clothes hanging around their waists, and he wasn't sure whether it was decent to look. Still, everyone else had gathered around to stare, so perhaps that sort of thing was acceptable in Paris.

Then he realized that, though the clothes hanging around her seemed crumpled like soft cloth, they had still been carved from the same solid stone as the rest of the statue. After that, he couldn't stop staring. How was it possible to take a lump of dead rock and make it look like it could ripple in the breeze, he wondered.

And then it finally dawned on him that something was missing. "Are her arms in another room, then?" he whispered to Ben, and couldn't understand why Ben was plainly trying not to laugh.

"Francis the First also began a new art collection at the Louvre," said Gaston. "He started with just twelve paintings but now we have more than two thousand. And in here we have the most famous of them all —"

"The *Mona Lisa*," declared Dominique.

Jack had no idea at all why Emily and Ben were so enthralled by the painting. It was not very big, and there was a tint over the whole thing that made it look as if it had been painted in a greenish haze. Jack was far more interested in the next item on Gaston's tour.

"Look here," said Gaston. They were standing in what had once been a sitting room with a view over the gardens below. Portraits of ladies and gentlemen hung from the ornately paneled walls. The guide rested his hand casually against the carved mantelpiece of a grand fireplace, which was surrounded by the ornate wooden wall panels. "This is an ordinary room, is it not?" he asked.

The three English friends looked around and agreed that it seemed like an ordinary room. "An ordinary room for a *palace*," Jack muttered.

"But you see this carving here?" Gaston continued with a broad smile. He tapped his fingers on the carving in question. "The monogram of Louis the Thirteenth? Well . . ."

"You press it and it opens," said Dominique, demonstrating. A section of the paneling around the fireplace swung open to reveal a dark rectangular alcove.

"You press it and it opens," Gaston muttered, the suspense ruined.

Ben, Emily, and Jack peered curiously into the dark cubbyhole.

"It is said that Cardinal Richelieu would invite his enemies here," said Gaston with a grin. "They would sit in this room and await the cardinal. An assassin would hide in the secret chamber here until the coast was clear, then emerge to kill the cardinal's guest! The murder was discovered, but by then the assassin was hidden again. And he would remain so until everyone had gone away."

"It is horrible," Dominique said with a shudder. "I am sure it is full of spiders."

"Hope so," Jack murmured, receiving another glare from Emily and another soft punch from Ben.

They returned to the vicomte's office in the late afternoon as the sun sank low on the horizon. Adensnap and the vicomte were sprawled in comfortable chairs, still talking happily.

"Ah. You are back," the vicomte said. He smiled but did not sound especially pleased to see them again. "Were you well looked after?"

"Very well, sir," Ben replied.

"Good, good," said Adensnap. "Now, listen, my friends. I need to prepare for my address to the symposium, and Henri has kindly offered to let us all stay with him."

"I have plenty of room," the vicomte put in. "I am sure you young people will have plenty to talk about."

"So I will stay here and work for a bit while you go home with the vicomte. How does that sound?" asked the professor.

Jack could tell the vicomte was hoping they would keep Dominique amused. It was not a task that appealed to him. He suspected that Ben and Emily were thinking exactly the same thing.

"Our bags are checked in at the hotel, Professor," Emily pointed out.

"Not to worry, not to worry," Adensnap said cheerfully. "I'll collect them myself on my way back later. You go along with Henri now."

So the friends had no choice but to follow the vicomte and Dominique out of the office.

So far Jack had not been impressed by the vicomte. Despite his stylish suit, Jack thought the Frenchman looked remarkably normal for a member of the aristocracy. He had been hoping for a long cloak, perhaps a wig or even a small crown.

But Jack's opinion began to change when he saw the vicomte's personal coach—a luxurious cream-and-gold four-wheeler with a coat of arms on the door. It was pulled by a pair of elegant gray horses and driven by a splendid coachman who sat up in the driver's seat, wrapped in a thick coat and top hat. *This*, Jack thought, *was more like it.*

"Home, with all haste," the vicomte said curtly to the driver, who had descended to hold the door open for him. The driver nodded, waited for them all to climb in, and then ascended to his own seat once more. The coach set off with a jerk.

The vicomte, Jack suspected, was a man who had never had to ask for anything. And it showed. Jack had had to ask for—or beg, or steal—a great deal in his life. He knew a little politeness went a long way. Clearly the vicomte had never needed to learn that himself.

The vicomte lived in an elegant La Chapelle mansion. Its sweeping, graveled drive and stuccoed exterior were a world away from Professor Adensnap's small house in Paddington.

"Of course, Uncle Henri's château at Montargis is far bigger," said Dominique. "And so is Mama's villa in Toulon. It has over one hundred rooms—Montargis, I mean, not Toulon.

I have lived there all my life—Toulon, I mean, not Montargis. It is very near the sea and I love to walk on the beach—except when the sea comes in. And I do not like crabs, but the sailors are very funny. We sometimes visit Marseilles and it is full of them—sailors, I mean, not crabs, though there are lots of those, too, but only on sale in the market. . . ."

"How . . . interesting, Dominique," Emily said politely. Jack, Ben, and the vicomte exchanged glances, then looked away, happy to leave Emily to cope with Dominique's chatter.

The vicomte's housekeeper was a small, plump woman who welcomed the three unexpected young guests and hurried away to ensure that rooms were prepared for them. Ben and Jack were to share a room, while Emily was to share Dominique's.

The gong struck at seven o'clock sharp, and the four children were ushered into the dining room, where the evening meal was laid out on a table of dark, polished wood. Gaslights on the walls and a roaring fire in the grate cast a warm, welcoming glow over the room. Deep red velvet curtains were drawn against the October chill, and the food filled the room with tantalizing scents.

The three English friends gazed hungrily at a small feast of stuffed partridges, quail's eggs, and candied fruits.

"I apologize for such humble fare," the vicomte said sadly as they took their seats. "It is the best my incompetent staff could manage at short notice."

"It all looks delicious, sir," Ben assured his host, digging in eagerly.

Jack took an incautious gulp of what he assumed to be some kind of fruit juice and nearly choked when it turned out to be wine.

The vicomte thumped him on the back, which really didn't help. "It is stronger than the wine you have at home, no?" he said.

"What wine?" Jack wheezed. He wiped his streaming eyes and reached for a glass of water. Once he could breathe again, he became aware of Dominique prattling across the table.

"Dear Emily, you have to tell me about the fashions in London, because I notice your blouse has two frills on it, but mine has four, and I think four is more becoming, but it might be different in London. I also have a lovely blue dress with pleats in it that I would show you—but it is in Toulon. Once I spilled some sauces on it and my mother was most upset, but they soon cleaned off, I mean the sauces, not the pleats, and . . ."

Jack and Ben glanced at each other and grinned.

Dominique paused for a sip of water, and Emily seized the opportunity to talk to the vicomte. "Sir, on the way here Professor Adensnap told us about your work on the Mayan calendar."

The vicomte paused in surprise, a spoon halfway to his mouth. He put the spoon down again. "Well, yes, I have made some contributions in that area," he said. "I have to warn you, it is a complex subject. . . ."

Jack could guess what he meant: *and not easy for girls to understand.* He was sure Emily realized what the vicomte was thinking, too, because she smiled.

"I understand you concluded that the calendar uses three different systems, all at the same time?" she said. "The long count, the divine calendar, and the civil calendar?"

The vicomte raised both eyebrows. "Well! Alfred told me you had helped his researches, but I had no idea you were so well informed. Yes, Emily, it is as you say. For a long time no one could understand the ancient Mayan calendar because we had assumed it was like ours—based on just one system. Once I realized it was actually based on three separate systems, the rest was surprisingly easy."

Jack nudged Ben, and Ben grinned triumphantly. They had clearly gone up in the vicomte's estimation. But then Dominique seemed to realize she had lost her audience and turned her attention to the boys.

"Ben, Jack, do all boys in England dress like you? Because I have a cousin in Nice whose coats are much longer. They come almost to the knees, and the lapels are wider—which is useful if you have a large cravat, as the proportions around the neck are kept similar. He has a particular coat that he is very fond of—made of silk—and once our cat jumped on it, and he had his claws out—the cat, I mean, not my cousin—and my cousin had it thrown away—I mean the coat, not the cat. . . ."

Jack sighed and got on with the business of eating.

After the meal they withdrew to the drawing room. The vicomte produced a box of cigars and offered them to Ben and Jack. They stared and couldn't quite summon the courage to take a cigar each before the vicomte took it back. "Oh, well. Perhaps you are a little young." He took one himself and lit it from a candle. Then he rang the bell for coffee, and he and Emily carried on discussing the ancient Mayan civilization.

Dominique introduced Ben and Jack to the delights of gin rummy, taking them on one at a time and beating them both easily, until they began to get the hang of it and could fight back. She laughed and clapped her hands at every victory, even when she lost, and the evening was far more enjoyable than Jack had thought it would be.

At last the clock on the mantelpiece struck ten in clear ringing chimes.

"Ten o'clock already?" said the vicomte. "Alas, I think it is time for bed."

Ben and Jack lay in their beds, on either side of a large bay window. Moonlight glowed through the curtains and gave the room a silvery hue.

"Talkative, ain't she?" Jack murmured. They could just hear Dominique's high-pitched voice through the wall. She seemed to be chatting about nightdresses.

Ben laughed. "Maybe she'll talk Em to sleep," he said. "Anyway, the professor's symposium will start soon, and then I doubt we'll see much of her. I get the impression she's not much interested in archaeology."

Jack had almost forgotten his particular reason for coming to Paris. In spite of his fears regarding Camazotz and the vampire plague, he had enjoyed the evening. He had allowed himself to relax. Now he felt tension return. "The prof hasn't turned up," he pointed out.

"You know him when he's busy." Ben yawned. "He'll be there till midnight and think it's only six in the evening."

"Yeah, I know, but . . ." Jack bit his tongue to stop himself. After the embarrassment in the station waiting room, he had resolved to believe Emily and Ben and try to accept that Camazotz was gone. *No, he ain't,* said a small part of his mind, *so stop fooling yourself!*

Jack propped himself up on one elbow and glanced out the window at the lights of Paris. His first full night in a foreign land, and everything was just the same as it had been in England. He believed Camazotz was still at large, Ben didn't, and they were never going to agree on it. "Yeah," he said. "G'night, Ben."

But Ben was already asleep. Jack stayed awake for much longer.

Chapter Eight

Jack woke early. In fact, he didn't remember sleeping. He supposed he must have, but he was awake when the first light of dawn started to show dimly through the curtains. And he heard the first cries of the Paris street traders as the day's business got under way.

Jack swung his legs out of bed and got up. He pulled his clothes on and splashed water from a bowl onto his face. On the other side of the room, Ben was still breathing softly in the steady rhythm of sleep. Jack slipped out onto the landing.

A maid was down in the front hall, drawing the curtains. Daylight splashed onto the tiles as Jack ambled down the stairs. The bell rang, and the maid hurried to open the door.

"*Bonjour, Pierre. Ça va?*" she asked pleasantly. *Good morning, Pierre. How are you?* Like all the French people Jack had met, the maid seemed to speak far too fast and the words ran together in his head, but he could just about understand the conversation so far.

Pierre, Jack saw, was the baker's boy, and a few years older than himself. The lad was making the daily delivery, handing the girl three or four long, thin loaves of bread. She gave him a few coins in return, and Pierre chatted easily as they made this exchange. Jack could only understand a few words. "*Louvre . . . terrible . . .*"

"What about the Louvre?" he demanded sharply in English, suddenly alarmed. They hadn't seen him there, halfway down the stairs, and they both jumped. The maid started to explain in French, but Jack couldn't understand properly. He turned and ran back upstairs.

The professor's room was across the hall from his own. He threw the door open and peered in. The bed was still neatly made. It hadn't been slept in.

"Jack? What is it?" Emily was now up and dressed, and she had seen Jack's mad rush to the professor's guest room as she had been coming out of her own.

"Something's happened at the Louvre," Jack gasped, "and the prof didn't come back last night. We got to get there —"

Emily held a finger to her lips. "Dominique's still asleep," she warned, and carefully closed the bedroom door behind her. She turned back to Jack. "You can't jump to conclusions, Jack," she said reasonably. "He might have worked late and then decided to go to the hotel rather than wake the whole household."

"Yeah, maybe, but Camazotz —" Jack started, breaking off as he remembered that Emily would just think him paranoid.

She was looking at him with resigned patience. "You

really are worried, aren't you, Jack?" she said quietly. "You really do believe that Camazotz is here?"

"Yes, and we got to —" Jack began urgently.

This time Emily held a finger to *his* lips. "It can't hurt to check, if it will set your mind at rest," she said, surprising him with her understanding. "You get Ben up. I'll find out all I can from the maid."

"Why do we have to go back to the museum?" Dominique grumbled as the vicomte's private coach rattled through the streets of Paris. "I was so looking forward to showing Emily the new fashions."

Outside, the air was damp and chilly, and wisps of fog drifted up from the river. The coach moved as briskly as the fog and the traffic would allow, but Ben could see it was still too slow for Jack's liking. His friend was drumming his fingers impatiently on the seat.

"The bread boy said there had been a break-in," explained the vicomte, with barely concealed impatience. "I need to investigate, and I cannot leave you all alone. You will have to wait, my dear."

"I hate waiting," Dominique muttered. "It is most inconvenient. It is like the time when I had seen a new scarf in the market, and I had my heart set on it, but I could not go to buy it at once because the coachman had been told by my father to wash the coach down, as he had been out hunting the day before—my father, that is, not the coachman. And, of course, he did not take the coach hunting because that would be foolish. I mean, how would you get it over the hedges? But . . ."

At last, the coach clattered into the Place du Carrousel and drew to a halt at the grand entrance of the Louvre.

"*Monsieur! Monsieur le Vicomte!*" babbled one of the doormen as they stepped out of the coach. "*Quelle tragédie affreuse . . .*"

Ben didn't wait to find out what the tragedy was. He was suddenly struck by the awful thought that Jack might be right. He broke into a run, dashing past the doorman and into the museum, ignoring the cries that told him to stop. Emily and Jack weren't far behind.

They heard other footsteps in pursuit but they didn't care. They pelted along the Grande Galerie and through the many halls and corridors of the Louvre. Finally they came to a halt at the South American gallery and stared around in horror.

The gallery had been ransacked. Shattered glass lay everywhere. Display cases had been knocked to the ground, their contents scattered across the polished wooden floor. Museum staff were picking their way carefully through the mess, trying to restore some kind of order.

"The professor's not here," Emily said.

"He would have been working in the office," Ben replied, and broke into a run again.

A gendarme lounged outside the door to the vicomte's

office. He straightened up when he saw Ben coming and held up a hand. "*Non!*" he declared, but Ben ducked under his arm and pushed the door open.

The office was in the wildest disorder, the furniture broken and the pieces scattered about the room. The drawers of the desk had been pulled open and thoroughly rifled. But, most disturbing of all, a sheet was laid out over a body on the floor. The face was covered, but Ben immediately recognized the professor's umbrella, which had been snapped in two, and his shoes, which poked out from one end of the sheet.

The three friends sat on a sofa at one side of the gallery, united in their grief. Museum attendants worked silently around them, trying to restore the gallery to its proper state. Ben had his arm around Emily. He could feel her trembling as they leaned against each other.

"He can't be dead, he can't be, he can't be," she kept whispering.

Jack had his head in his hands, and Ben sat silently, biting his lip and staring into the distance. His mind was whirling, searching for possibilities—anything that would mean the professor wasn't lying dead in the vicomte's office.

"My deepest sympathies." The vicomte stood over them, his face drawn. Ben saw that Dominique was standing a little apart, waiting for her uncle. "I have identified poor Alfred's body. It is a tragedy. And . . ." He turned to the wrecked gallery and gestured sadly. "And *this*!" He shook his head. "Some *animal* has killed Alfred and done all this damage."

"*Monsieur le Vicomte?*" said a tall, thin man, coming up behind him. "I am Isidore Muset of the gendarmerie."

"Ah," said the vicomte. "Perhaps you can tell us what has happened?"

"There is little to say," the man replied with an apologetic shrug. "This atrocity occurred in the wee hours. It was discovered when the museum opened. We sent someone to fetch you, sir, but you were already on your way here. It is a strange incident. You kept a large sum of gold coins in your desk?" The vicomte nodded. "They were spilled on the floor when the intruder searched the desk, but they were not taken. It is very odd, is it not?"

The three friends looked at one another. They were not surprised to learn that whoever had done this had not been interested in money.

"Indeed, nothing at all seems to have been taken," the gendarme went on. "And yet, there has been this savage destruction. We assume your friend, the professor, disturbed the perpetrator and was, therefore, murdered." He swallowed. "I am afraid he was killed in a most upsetting manner."

The three friends just looked at him, waiting for him to continue—and confirm their worst suspicions.

"I do not think we should upset these young people with such details —" the vicomte began.

"No, please," Ben interrupted him. "Please, sir. We need to know."

Muset glanced at the vicomte, then back at Ben. He put his hand to his throat. "He seems to have been *bitten*," he said. "The professor's throat was almost torn out. And his body was drained of blood. Perhaps he was already suffering from this strange illness—this plague that sweeps Paris. Or perhaps the two things are connected in some way."

Ben shut his eyes. He felt Emily lean heavily against him, and Jack bowed his head and let out a long, slow breath. It was just as they had feared.

The gendarme shook his head and went on in a murmur, as if thinking out loud. "Ordinary assassins do not use such methods. This butchery without motive, it is grotesque."

"Yes, yes," said the vicomte. "It is obvious that a madman has done this deed. A maniac, escaped from a neighboring maison de santé—an asylum. Thank you, monsieur."

The gendarme bowed and took his leave.

"Sir," Ben said quietly, "may we have some time to ourselves? We need to talk."

"Of course." The vicomte bowed graciously. "Take as long as you like. Let me know when you are ready."

They watched him walk away to join his niece, and Ben turned to Jack. His worst fears had taken shape, and he knew there was something he had to say to his friend before anything else.

"Jack." It came out almost as a whisper and he had to try again. "Jack," he said more loudly. Jack lifted his head and looked at him dully. "I . . . I am so sorry I didn't believe you. I was such an idiot. I so badly wanted to believe Camazotz was gone, and you tried to warn us, but . . ."

"It wasn't just you, Ben," Emily put in, her voice shaking slightly. "I was just as bad. Jack, we both owe you a huge apology."

"Don't worry," Jack muttered. Ben saw him flush slightly and thought that, though sometimes Jack could be shameless, at other times he was easily embarrassed. "The prof's dead and we got a problem to deal with. That's all that matters," Jack finished.

"Yes, you're right," Emily agreed. And suddenly her voice was much firmer. "We *do* have a problem—a problem that wouldn't be here if we'd dealt with it properly in the first place. If Camazotz and his vampires are still around, then we will have to find another way to vanquish them once and for all!" She almost spat out those last words. She had gone from the depths of grief to focused fury in a matter of seconds.

Ben wasn't used to seeing his sister like this. "Yes, we must," he agreed more quietly. "But that means we will have to stay in France. And we don't have a guardian anymore. The professor was meant to be looking after us."

"Don't need the prof to do that," Jack remarked.

"No, but the law might not agree," Ben pointed out.

"We'll just have to manage," Emily said flatly. Her mind was obviously made up. "Defeating Camazotz has to come first."

"Yes, but how do we go about it?" Ben asked thoughtfully. "Last time, we had the professor's help. If we're to have any chance of success this time, we need someone with a similar knowledge of the Maya. Someone, well . . ." He nodded across the gallery to where the vicomte was directing the staff as they tried to set his department to rights.

Jack followed his gaze. "Wait a moment!" he said. "He don't seem like the sort of bloke who will believe a story like ours."

"We'll just have to be convincing," said Ben. "The professor believed us, eventually, because he knew what we said made sense. The vicomte is a scientist, too. He won't *want* to believe us—the professor didn't, either—so we must find a way to present the evidence and make it impossible for him to disagree."

"Maybe we can ask him about the eye," Jack said slowly. Ben and Emily looked at him questioningly. "Weren't it made by the same bloke as made the gold bat? And we know Camazotz were after that. Maybe Camazotz—or one of 'is servants—was looking for it last night. Maybe the prof just got in the way."

"Maybe," said Emily, frowning as she considered this idea. "Yes, you could be right."

"Then we're agreed," Ben said resolutely. "We tell the vicomte."

"And if he won't help," Emily added grimly, "we'll just have to manage on our own."

Jack got slowly to his feet. "Well, let's find out, eh?"

Chapter Nine

"Sir," said Ben, "we would like to talk to you. We . . . we think we know something about the person who did this."

The vicomte turned slowly toward them. His eyes glittered behind his spectacles. "Young minds can be fanciful," he said. "Forgive me, but I doubt that three English youngsters can have much knowledge of the French criminal classes."

Ben swallowed and glanced at Emily and Jack. They both nodded encouragingly. He looked back at the vicomte. He remembered the time he had first told Professor Adensnap about the vampires. Then, too, he had felt anxious about telling such an outlandish tale to someone he barely knew. But the sophisticated vicomte was infinitely more intimidating than the affable Professor Adensnap.

The Frenchman was still looking at Ben, awaiting his response. Ben reminded himself that the vicomte knew everything the professor had known about the ancient Mayans. Adensnap had believed Ben's tale, simply because everything he had said fit with the historical facts and the Mayan mythology. The professor had been *reluctant* to believe the terrible truth, but he hadn't just dismissed it out of hand. Ben prayed that the vicomte's reaction would be the same. "We had an . . . enemy, in London," he began cautiously. "He killed people there, too, including my father."

He could see the vicomte beginning to take an interest.

"Please, sir," Ben continued, hoping that the Vicomte de Montargis could hear the sincerity in his voice, "just give us five minutes. But"— he shuddered —"somewhere else. Not here."

The vicomte inclined his head. "Very well," he said calmly. "Come with me."

A short trip in the vicomte's coach brought them to a tall, classical building off the Place Vendôme, not far from the Louvre. A massive arch framed the entrance, through which a flight of wide stone steps led into the building.

Inside, the air was hazy with cigar smoke. The friends found themselves standing in a wide hallway, the roof of which was supported by graceful wrought-iron pillars. A broad staircase swept away to the upper levels. Ben noticed that the noise from the street was muffled by thick red carpets and heavy tapestries that hung on the walls.

A spacious lounge opened off the lobby. It was full of men who looked like the vicomte—wealthy and stylishly dressed. Some held murmured conversations; others sat in comfortable armchairs, reading the papers. The vicomte, in his fifties, was one of the younger men there.

"Is this your club, sir?" Emily inquired.

The vicomte looked down at her, and for a moment there was a mischievous twinkle in his eye. "Not at all, mademoiselle," he replied. "Clubs are banned in France, under the laws forbidding association. This is simply a place where like-minded gentlemen such as myself can come to relax and escape the pressures of life—for a small fee toward the running costs, of course."

"Sounds like a club to me," Jack muttered.

The Frenchman smiled and patted him on the shoulder. "In Paris, Jack, we are skilled at saying one thing and meaning another. As long as everyone knows what is meant, we get along. This way . . ."

He led them down a side corridor and into a private sitting room. It was stuffy and windowless but empty. The only light came from gas lamps, their flickering glow reflected in a large mirror hanging above the fireplace opposite the door. Comfortable red leather chairs were scattered about the room.

The vicomte tugged a bellpull, and when a servant appeared, he ordered coffee for them all.

"And now," he said, turning to face Ben, "what is it you have to tell me?"

"Sir . . ." Ben began, casting a doubtful glance at

Dominique. He was just about willing to trust the vicomte with his extraordinary tale, but Dominique was another matter entirely.

The vicomte didn't hesitate. "Dominique," he said, "please wait outside."

"Oh, Uncle —" she began, then subsided when he glared at her. "Yes, Uncle Henri," she said meekly, and withdrew.

The vicomte settled down in a chair near the fire. "Pull up some chairs," he told the friends, "and tell me what it is you want to say."

"Well, sir." Ben took a deep breath. "I suppose it all started on our expedition to Mexico." And he told the vicomte the whole story. How, in Mexico, they had discovered a cave full of bats, not realizing until much later that it contained the banished vampire god, Camazotz, and his followers. How Camazotz had possessed Sir Donald Finlay, and his vampires had picked off the expedition members one by one. How Camazotz, in Sir Donald's body, had come to London and started the vampire plague that swept the city.

He also explained how he and Jack and Emily had met Professor Adensnap. How, with his help, they had found the blood rose. And how they had discovered the ritual that they had eventually used to banish the demon god, with his vampires, back to the hellfires from which they came.

When Ben had finished, the vicomte sat back in his chair and steepled his fingers together thoughtfully. Ben held his breath.

The vicomte raised his voice slightly. "Dominique!" he called. "You may come in now."

Dominique poked her head around the door.

"Thank you," her uncle said mildly. "Take a seat."

He looked at Ben, Jack, and Emily. "It is an inventive tale," he said. "But it is hardly helpful in the present situation."

They looked at him blankly. "Sir?" Ben queried.

"Benedict," the vicomte said firmly, "it is obvious that your tale is very real, inside your own heads. You are intelligent young people and there is no denying young Emily's depth of knowledge about matters concerning the ancient Mayan civilization. I can vouch for that myself. Now, I never thought I would say this, but perhaps young people can be *too* educated. Your learning has obviously led to this, this . . . *delusion* that the three of you share. Poor Alfred, sweet man that he was, no doubt humored you in it. But please, I beg you, learn to look beyond it. Look at what is real. You have all been hit by a terrible tragedy, but sheltering in a shared fantasy will do you no good."

"But, Vicomte, I swear it's true," Emily put in urgently. "You know the legends of Camazotz —"

"Of course I know the legends!" the vicomte exclaimed. "But I am a rational man. Camazotz was just a man — a terrible leader, a man of great evil, but *just* a man."

"Sir," Emily cried in despair. "You heard the professor say we had helped his researches."

"Yes, I did." He shook his head. "And I was most

impressed. But unfortunately you seem unable to distinguish between reality and this terrible illusion of yours."

Ben was aghast. "But, sir . . ."

"No!" The vicomte held up a hand. "I think it is best that you all return to England. I will make arrangements at once." There was a knock on the door. "*Qu'est-ce que c'est?*" called the vicomte.

The door opened and a servant entered the room. He wore a crisp white tunic and carried a silver tray laden with a coffeepot and cups.

"*Ah, bien,*" said the vicomte. To the friends he added, "We will say no more about this. You have had a terrible shock. May I offer you some refreshment?"

The servant set the tray down on a small table. He paused, looking from the friends to the vicomte.

"If it's all the same to you, sir," Ben said tightly, "we'll wait outside. We need to discuss . . . things."

"As you will," the vicomte replied with a shrug. "Dominique, you had better stay here."

Dominique looked at her uncle, then at the three friends, with a puzzled frown. She slowly sat down beside her uncle as the waiter poured her coffee.

Ben put one hand on his sister's arm. "Come on, Em," he said quietly, and they all moved toward the door.

"Stupid vicomte, thinks he knows it all!" Jack muttered in frustration. He took one last, bitter look back as he passed through the doorway and saw himself reflected in the mirror over the fireplace. He made a face at his reflection. But as he turned away, he noticed another face reflected in the mirror—the face of the waiter. And in the reflection, it was not at all as it should have been, for red eyes gazed back at Jack from a face distorted by vampire fangs.

Chapter Ten

Jack froze. He rubbed his eyes. He looked back at the room. The vicomte was sitting in his chair. Dominique was looking at her uncle. The servant was pouring the coffee. His face seemed quite normal, and Jack thought he must have imagined the hideous reflection.

But then the waiter straightened up and came into line with the mirror again. Jack saw that the man's reflection wore the same uniform, but his face was dark and twisted. His eyes blazed red, his ears were pointed, and his lips were pushed back by the vicious fangs protruding from his mouth.

Jack's hand flew to his pocket, where he had kept the tin with the blood rose. And then he remembered he didn't have it anymore.

"Vicomte!" Jack shouted—or, at least, tried to. The word came out as a hoarse croak. He raised a shaking hand and pointed at the mirror. "Look . . ." he whispered. Then he cleared his throat and said again, more loudly, "Look! The reflection!"

"Hmm?" The vicomte glanced casually behind him at the mirror and saw what Jack had seen. He leapt away from the servant with a shout of surprise.

The waiter immediately hissed and dropped the coffeepot. His mouth sprouted fangs, his eyes shone red, and his fingers turned into claws. He had become the creature that the mirror showed. The vicomte backed away from him.

"The master has need of you, Montargis," the vampire hissed.

"Jack!" the vicomte shouted desperately. "Take Dominique and get out of here!"

Dominique had risen from her chair, her eyes fixed on the vampire. She seemed transfixed in horror. The vicomte moved toward her, but the waiter blocked his way.

"What's happening?" Ben asked. He and Emily peered over Jack's shoulder, and their jaws dropped when they saw the vampire advancing on the vicomte.

As the vampire moved to attack her uncle, Dominique finally opened her mouth and screamed. The waiter hissed and spun to face her.

But Jack was already running forward. *If he couldn't help the vicomte*, he thought, *he could at least help Dominique.* He grabbed the girl and dragged her backward, just as the vampire lashed out at her with his claws. The sharp talons slashed easily through Dominique's coat but missed her flesh.

And then, quite unexpectedly, the vampire screamed

and drew back. He crouched with his hands over his face, as if he had been blinded by a dazzling light. For just a moment, he left space for the vicomte to get past.

The vicomte was a large man, but he made it to the other end of the room in seconds. Ben pulled him out into the corridor and Jack dragged Dominique after them. He shot a final, puzzled look at the vampire waiter, to see that he was already recovering from whatever had scared him.

Emily slammed the door shut. "It doesn't have a lock," she said.

"Then come on, quick," Ben replied, and set off quickly down the corridor. The noise had already drawn looks of disapproval from the other members. Ben didn't want to run and draw more attention, but he didn't want to linger near that room, either. The rest of the group followed him.

They were halfway down the corridor when the door to the room flew open. The waiter charged out, now in human form again. "You cannot flee!" he cried as he strode down the corridor toward them, pushing aside another member of the club.

"Well, really!" the old gentleman muttered as he was shouldered against the wall.

The vampire ignored him. "This city belongs to the master!" he shouted.

Dominique broke free of Jack as they reached the lobby and looked down at her ripped coat.

"It is *ruined*!" she wailed. "And it is my fav—"

"Come on!" Jack shouted. He grabbed the coat and

pulled. It came apart and he staggered back, clutching half of it in his hand as the vampire ran into the lobby after them. The remains of the coat fell to the floor in a heap, and the vampire screamed again. He cowered away from Dominique, his arms held up as if to ward her off.

"What's happening?" Jack murmured. The vampire was now backing down the corridor, away from them.

"Jack! Come on!" Ben shouted from behind him.

Jack kept his eyes on the waiter and saw that he stopped when he was about twenty feet away. "Come on, Dominique. You can always buy a new coat," Jack said. He took her hand and gently led her away toward the main doors. Slowly the vampire followed.

Dominique was watching. "He is frightened of something!" she said wonderingly. "But what?" She stopped, and so did the waiter. She took a step toward him.

"No, wait," Jack gasped, but the words died in his throat. The vampire had taken a step back as Dominique had moved toward him. She stepped forward again, and the vampire immediately retreated another step. She smiled triumphantly at Jack. "You see?" she said. "He is afraid of me!"

"Yes," Jack said. He saw it. He just couldn't believe it.

Ben, Emily, and the vicomte came slowly forward to join Dominique and Jack.

"Just now he was a monster. Now he is a man," Dominique commented. She looked back at the vampire. He was pacing about like a beast in a cage. He never took his eyes off the group, but he seemed unable to break through the invisible bars that kept him away from them.

"He's still a monster," Jack remarked grimly. "He drinks people's blood."

"If we leave, will he follow?" Dominique inquired.

"No. Vampires can't go out in direct sunlight and the sun is shining outside," Ben told her.

"But if he stays here, won't he hurt these people?" Dominique demanded.

"Um . . ." Jack glanced around at the club members. "Yes. He probably will."

Dominique shrugged. "Then we cannot leave him among all these people, can we?" she said. And she began to walk forward.

"No, Dom —" the vicomte commanded, but then he fell silent, for though the vampire hissed angrily, for some reason he couldn't bear to be close to her. Some mysterious force made him back away from the French girl, down the corridor, out of the lobby, and back the way he had come.

Another waiter came walking up the corridor behind the vampire. "Marc —" he began, putting a hand on the vampire's shoulder.

The vampire turned his head and hissed. The waiter caught a glimpse of the savage vampire fangs and backed away, trembling.

"Come, Jack!" Dominique called, and she suddenly charged at the vampire. The vampire staggered back, then turned and fled.

"Dominique, no!" Jack called. He had no choice but to follow her. The others ran after them both.

Jack chased Dominique and the vampire through a pair of swing doors at the end of the corridor and found himself in a large kitchen. A row of tables loaded with food and surrounded by chefs in grubby white overalls ran the length of the room.

The vampire was barging his way past the chefs toward one corner of the kitchen. Then he bent suddenly and pulled open a wooden trapdoor in the floor. Jack heard the sound of running water. The vampire crouched over the opening, glaring at Dominique. Then he hissed something at her in French—too fast for Jack's dockside education to follow—and dove below into the darkness.

Jack leapt forward and slammed the trapdoor shut. It had a bolt, which he threw across.

The chefs were huddled together, shouting and arguing, clearly shocked.

"Quiet!" said a commanding voice in French, from the doorway. The vicomte had entered the kitchen and Jack found that he had little trouble understanding the vicomte's precise speech. All eyes turned toward the French aristocrat. Jack knew that the vicomte had been shocked by the vampire, but there was no sign of it now. He stood before them calm, collected, and very much in control. "It was an escaped madman," he declared. "What else could it have been?"

"It looked like Marc," muttered someone.

"Yes, poor Marc, he is in the grip of madness!" the vicomte said regretfully.

"He didn't exactly look mad —" a chef began.

The vicomte turned on him. "And you are an expert on diseases of the mind? Hmm?" he demanded coldly.

The chef visibly quailed. "No, I am sorry, Monsieur le Vicomte. I would not presume . . ." he gabbled hastily.

"And what is the meaning of this disorder?" the vicomte asked, looking around the kitchen and clapping his hands together. "Back to work! There is no excuse for inefficiency."

Instantly the kitchen became a hive of cooking activity as everyone hurried back to work. The vicomte was used to being obeyed, and it did not occur to anyone to argue.

"You," said the vicomte to the head chef. "Where does that door lead?" He pointed at the trapdoor.

"To the sewers, sir," replied the head chef. "It is where we throw the scraps and waste."

"Well, keep it locked until the authorities arrive."

The head chef agreed that he would. He seemed anxious not to encounter Marc again. The vicomte nodded in satisfaction and turned away.

"Jack," Ben said, "the coach is outside. Come on."

"But did you see that vampire run from Dominique?" Jack asked eagerly.

"Yes, I saw it," Ben agreed. "Now let's go somewhere safe where we can discuss it."

Chapter Eleven

"*Mon Dieu!*" the vicomte whispered as he fell back into his seat in the coach. The confident display of authority he had managed in front of the kitchen staff was gone. His face was gray and anxious as he looked at the three friends, sitting opposite.

"*Now* will you listen?" Jack asked.

"Oh, yes, Uncle Henri," Dominique put in eagerly from beside her uncle. Her eyes shone and her face lit up as she looked over at Jack. "Listen to Jack! Listen to the one who saved my life! *Il faut que vous écoutez à mon chevalier anglais bien courageux!*"

Ben saw Jack frown and his lips move silently as he tried to translate Dominique's words.

Eventually he gave up. "What was that?" Jack whispered to Ben.

"'Listen to my brave English knight,'" Ben quoted, and in spite of everything that had happened, he couldn't help smiling.

"Who?" Jack began, and then, as Ben's grin widened, "*Me?* No!" he exclaimed in horror.

"Benedict, I owe you an apology," the vicomte said. It was a strange echo of Ben and Emily's apology to Jack earlier. The vicomte sounded almost resentful, as if his owing Ben an apology were Ben's fault. Ben guessed that apologizing was not something the Vicomte de Montargis had had to do very often. "Let me buy us all lunch, and we can discuss this further. I know just the place," the Frenchman said, and he rapped on the roof of the coach. "Lafarge," he ordered the driver.

The coach carried them swiftly up the hill to Montmartre, the high ground to the north of Paris. Inside the coach the atmosphere was drawn and tense, but outside there was laughter in the air.

Jack looked out the window. It was only midday but the streets were filling up with the kind of life he had always associated with evening. There was music and dancing, and as they passed open doors or windows he heard snatches of song and bursts of laughter from within.

The coach slowed as it picked its way through the crowd. Jack saw women in fancy dresses of rainbow colors and men in top hats and coats of reds and greens and golds. A clown on stilts moved slowly through the throng, juggling as he went. A clever trick, Jack had to admit, but he couldn't really see the point. Then someone threw the clown a coin, which the man caught and dropped into a pocket without breaking the rhythm of his juggling. Jack knew what poverty was like. Any trick that earned money had a point to it.

The streets were lined with bars and cafés, and patrons sat out on the pavement, enjoying the autumn sunshine. Jack found it hard to tell where one establishment ended and another began.

"We are here," the vicomte declared suddenly, and the coach came to a halt.

The friends could immediately see why the vicomte had chosen this particular restaurant. A mirror took up one entire wall. And sunlight flooded inside, making the place seem bright and airy and, above all, safe.

The maître d' knew the Vicomte de Montargis and offered him his usual table. It was in the middle of the room and the vicomte turned it down. Instead he took them to a table situated in a pool of sunshine, where he could sit with his back to the wall and keep an eye on anyone who approached. When a waiter or a customer drew near, he looked carefully at their reflection in the mirror.

The others sat down around the table. Jack was uncomfortably aware that Dominique had chosen to sit right beside him. Out of the corner of his eye he was sure he could see her staring at him. He glanced at her to make sure, and immediately her face brightened. Jack quickly looked away again.

A waiter came to take their orders, then hurried off to the kitchen.

"Well," said the vicomte briskly, "tell me your story again, Benedict. Leave nothing out." He pulled a small notebook and a pencil out of his coat and looked expectantly at Ben.

Ben began his tale again. This time, the vicomte paid close attention, stopping Ben many times to ask a question or to clarify something.

"Once Camazotz had possessed Sir Donald, why did he not just slaughter all of you?" the vicomte asked.

"He needed humans as food for his vampires on the journey to the coast," Ben explained grimly. "My father and I were safe because we had a tent to sleep in at night. A vampire cannot enter a private residence, not even a tent, without permission."

"But Camazotz was able to board the ship?" the vicomte demanded.

"Only after he made the captain ask him on board," Ben replied.

"Well, how did Camazotz hear of the statue in the British Museum?"

"Once he possessed Sir Donald, he knew everything Sir Donald knew," Ben replied. He understood that the vicomte was just being thorough, but Ben had the feeling he was being tested, too. The vicomte wanted to find a flaw in his story—an excuse to believe things were not as bad as they seemed.

Finally Ben had brought the vicomte up to date with everything they knew. Dominique, who was hearing this story for the first time, looked amazed—and was even more impressed with Jack.

Her uncle shook his head sadly. "Poor Alfred," he said. "He must have thought the vampires were gone, too, and then . . ." He looked suddenly alarmed. "There is no chance that Alfred has become one of them?"

"No, sir," Emily reassured him. "They . . ." She took a moment to compose herself, and Ben gave her hand a squeeze. "They left his body behind. They just killed him."

"It takes three bites from a vampire to change you," Ben added.

"Well, thank God for that," the vicomte said with a shudder. "But why would he send one of his servants for me at my club?"

"I think he wants your knowledge," Emily replied. "He either wanted to abduct you or change you into a vampire. Either way he would know what you know."

The vicomte shuddered again. "Then I am doubly grateful to you. But I confess I do not understand why the creature suddenly backed away."

"No," Ben said, and looked at the others. "We don't know that, either."

The vicomte sat back and sighed. "Then let us go through what we *do* know." He checked his notes. "Vampires can be killed with the blood rose. . . ."

"They can't stand sunlight on their skin," Ben added. "It burns them."

"And they can't enter a private home unless they are invited," Emily put in.

The vicomte nodded. "I will tell my housekeeper to admit no one unless I am there to vouch for them. And, let us not forget, we also know that a mirror reflects the vampire's true form. This I have seen for myself!"

"Yes, sir," Ben agreed. "We only discovered that today ourselves."

"But did you not hear what the vampire said before it dove into the sewers?" Dominique asked.

"What *did* he say?" Jack queried. "It were too quick for me to catch."

"He said, 'The master will have you. You cannot hide behind that trinket forever,'" answered Dominique.

"I wonder what trinket he meant. Dominique, what are you wearing today?" the vicomte asked.

All eyes turned to Dominique. She flushed but looked pleased to be the center of attention. "Well, my coat came from London, but it is ruined now. My blouse is silk, of course, and the buttons are inset with —"

"I meant, what jewelry are you wearing?" the vicomte interrupted gently. "What ornamentation?"

"Oh." Dominique thought for a moment. "Perhaps this?" From among the frills that ran down the front of her blouse, she drew a small pendant—a square of stone that hung around her neck on a thin gold chain. She held it up for them to see.

"Yeah, it could be that!" Jack said. "Remember the vampire jumped back when he cut Dominique's coat open."

"And then again when you pulled the coat off," Ben added. "He would have seen Dominique's medallion on both occasions. What exactly is it?"

They all leaned forward to look at it more closely. It was a small square inch of carved black stone in a gold mount. The stone was covered with glyphs that Jack recognized immediately. "They're Mayan," he said.

The vicomte was also peering closely through his spectacles. "Yes," he said. "I had the mount made when I gave the stone to Dominique for Christmas. The stone was brought back from the New World by Dampierre. He believed it to be some form of talisman connected with the Mayan god Chac."

"Chac!" Ben exclaimed. "That would make sense! It was Chac's followers who forced Camazotz into banishment."

"Well, well." The vicomte sat back again. "Chac, the god of rain and lightning. His rain brought life to the land and his lightning brought light into darkness. Life and light—two things Camazotz detests. I never thought to find an ally in a Mayan god whose worshippers died out a thousand years ago, but I am glad I have. The servants of Camazotz cannot, apparently, face a talisman of Chac. How interesting."

"Do you have any more of these at the museum, sir?" Ben inquired.

The vicomte shook his head regretfully. "Alas, no. They may be more common in Mexico, where Dampierre found this, but in France this is one of a kind. Dominique, you must take great care of it."

"Oh, Uncle Henri, I will!" Dominique stared at the talisman in wonder, then carefully tucked it back into her blouse.

"Now tell me again," the vicomte said, turning to Ben, "about this banishment you performed. We need to know why it didn't work."

He listened, taking more notes, as Ben described the ritual. The words and instructions had come from an ancient manuscript known to Professor Adensnap. The friends had found the vital ingredient, the blood rose, at Kew Gardens, and then they had brewed the potion, thrown it over Camazotz, and chanted a powerful incantation. The ritual had *seemed* to work.

"The potion wasn't quite pure," Emily pointed out hesitantly.

The vicomte looked interested. "Not pure? Why not?"

"Camazotz was controlling my mind," Ben explained shortly. "He made me pour the potion away—onto the ground. But Jack and I threw the damp earth at Camazotz, and Emily recited the incantation. It seemed to have the desired effect."

The vicomte shrugged. "Perhaps it did. But it is possible the earth diluted the potion and hence its power. Or that Emily's Mayan accent was not quite up to scratch.

Or any one of a hundred other things. In any case, we know that the ritual was only partly successful. And we know that without the blood rose, there is no hope of repeating it. Hmm . . ." He ran his eye down the notes and tapped at a particular line. "Tell me more about Sherwood's statue," he said. "I have heard of it, of course. But I have never seen it."

"Our godfather, Edwin Sherwood, brought it back from Mexico some years ago," Ben said. "It was a bat standing on its hind feet like a man. It stood about six inches high and its wings were outstretched. It was solid gold. Camazotz stole it from the British Museum. We saw it on his altar, with something else—a small gold crown, the same sort of size."

The vicomte took off his pince-nez and pinched the bridge of his nose thoughtfully. "And did you ever learn why Camazotz wanted it?" he asked.

"Um, no, sir," Ben replied.

The vicomte gazed at the ceiling. "You saw the damage in the museum. The place was ransacked. I would deduce Camazotz was searching for something —"

"The eye," said Jack. The vicomte looked back at him.

"Exactly, Jack. The eye. Dampierre believed it to have been made by the same craftsman who made the bat. Camazotz may be searching for objects made by this craftsman." He sighed. "In which case, poor Alfred's death is indeed a tragic waste."

The friends stared at him.

"What do you mean, sir?" asked Emily.

He shrugged. "I mean that if Camazotz was looking for the eye last night, he would never have found it in the Louvre, for it was not there."

"Where was it?" Ben asked slowly.

"It was in the same place as you, Benedict. It was at my house, and it still is."

Chapter Twelve

"Privacy is sometimes hard to come by at the museum," said the vicomte as they walked up the steps to his mansion. The housekeeper and the butler were waiting for them by the door, like sentries standing on duty. The vicomte threw his coat and hat for the butler to catch and swept on into his study without breaking step. The others hurried after him.

"Sometimes I want to work without being disturbed. If I need solitude, I will bring certain objects home with me for further study. It is not really permitted for anyone to remove items from the museum—even temporarily—but I am the Vicomte de Montargis," he said with a shrug, as if that explained everything. Clearly, being an aristocrat had its privileges. "I brought the eye back here a few days ago."

The study was light and airy, with gilt decoration around the fireplace and gold curtains at the windows. The vicomte opened a desk and withdrew a tray on which something lay wrapped in a red cloth. He laid the tray on a table. The four children crowded around to look as he uncovered the eye.

Like the bat, the eye was solid gold and roughly the size of a small plate. Jack had been expecting something round and smooth, like a real human eye, but the edges were square and angular, in the Mayan style. The pupil that stared out from the center was square, too, but still it seemed to glare at them with a cold, dead anger.

"May I?" asked Emily, reaching for it.

"Well . . ." began the vicomte, sounding reluctant. But Emily had already picked up the eye reverently. The front was smooth, apart from the carving of the pupil and the rim of the eye. But the back was covered with the organic pictures and shapes of Mayan hieroglyphics. There was also a curved groove down one side. Jack looked at it thoughtfully as Emily turned it over and over in her hands. It reminded him of something.

"Do you know what it is for, Uncle Henri?" Dominique asked.

"Sadly, no, my dear. But I guess it was made to be worn. See here." The vicomte took the eye gently from Emily and ran his fingers down the curved groove Jack had noticed. A small row of loops stuck out from the gold. A similar row of loops ran along the bottom edge. "You could put thread through these and attach it to someone. Or something."

Jack looked more closely. "Emily," he said, "have you got a picture of the bat statue?"

"I think so." Emily rummaged in her bag. She pulled out a piece of paper and gave it to Jack, who smoothed it out on the tabletop.

It was a sketch in black ink that Professor Adensnap had drawn. The statue seemed to rear up out of the paper, its wings spread as if to launch an attack.

"This drawing is the same size as the statue?" Jack queried.

"Yes, it's exactly life-size," Emily replied, looking at him curiously.

Jack took the eye from the vicomte and laid it down next to the drawing. The bat's right wing exactly overlaid the curved groove in the eye.

"*Mon Dieu!*" the vicomte exclaimed. "That cannot be a coincidence."

"See?" Jack said. "You could tie them together."

The vicomte groaned. "Alfred and I could have worked that out in seconds, if we had ever had both items in the same room together. Well done, Jack."

"Yes, Jack, well done," Dominique said, smiling proudly at him across the table. Jack flushed and looked away.

"Why stop at two pieces?" asked Emily. The eye lay on the table next to the drawing of the bat and she pointed at the bottom row of loops. "Something else could be attached down here."

"Something like a small gold crown?" Ben suggested quietly, remembering the golden artifacts that had been sitting on Camazotz's altar in London. The bat and the crown—Camazotz had taken them both with him.

They all looked down at the tabletop, filling in the missing crown with their imaginations. If the crown was a third piece, it left a very obvious blank. The three pieces together formed three quarters of a circle. A fourth piece was needed to complete the shape.

"So what goes here?" Jack said, tapping the empty space where a final, fourth piece could go.

The vicomte swore suddenly, in French. He used words that Ben and Emily's education had omitted. But Jack had learned his French at the docks and he looked at the vicomte in surprise. Dominique turned pale.

"You ask what goes there, Jack?" said the vicomte when he had finally recovered. "I think you will find it is a crescent moon."

The others looked at one another, then at him.

"How do you know that, Uncle Henri?" asked Dominique.

The vicomte pulled up a chair and sat down in it with his face in his hands. "There is an old manuscript at the museum," he said. "One of many. It is covered with hieroglyphics that we cannot translate, but it also has four very distinct images on it. Two of them are definitely a bat and an eye. And you have just reminded me of the third—it is some kind of headdress, or *crown*. I never connected them before, because of course I did not know about the crown that you say Camazotz already has. But now we know that three of the golden artifacts match three of those images, and if there are four in total . . . then, as I say, the fourth is a crescent moon."

"And you've only just remembered this?" Jack demanded.

The vicomte looked up at him and shrugged. "What difference does it make? We cannot translate the manuscript. No one has yet deciphered the ancient Mayan hieroglyphs to a sufficient degree. The document is a curiosity, nothing more."

"What do you mean?" Jack demanded. But then he remembered. *He* knew perfectly well that Ben and Emily's late father had worked out how to do just that—translate ancient Mayan hieroglyphics. And Emily had followed his notes and was now becoming skilled in doing so herself. But nobody else knew! Jack looked at Emily.

"Shall I tell him?" Emily asked the boys with a smile. Jack grinned and Ben simply bowed.

Emily turned to the vicomte, who was looking at them all as if they were mad. "Sir," she said, "you should take us to the Louvre quickly. I think I can help you with that translation."

Chapter Thirteen

They left the eye at the vicomte's house. After much deliberation, they all agreed that his home was the safest place to keep it. Where vampires were concerned, a private home was a safe that could not be cracked.

The vicomte's coach took them to the museum, where they found the South American gallery much tidier than it had been a few hours earlier. The display cases had been set upright again and the broken glass swept away. But a small army of museum staff was still at work setting things to rights, and a gendarme still stood guard outside the passage that led to the vicomte's office.

"Wait here," the vicomte said, and went over to talk to the policeman. After a moment he beckoned them over, and they all realized he had been checking that Professor Adensnap's body no longer lay in his office. It was a sad reminder that their battle with the Mayan vampire god was far from over.

The office faced south and sunlight streamed in through the large bay window. It made the place slightly more cheerful, although the room was chilly—no one had closed the window that led out onto the balcony. Papers were scattered everywhere, drawers had been yanked open, their contents spilled onto the ground, and the books were in complete disarray.

"I told them I would tidy up myself," the vicomte said. "I need to maintain my system. Wait a moment." He turned to one of the filing cabinets and pulled open a drawer. It was empty. He grimaced and bent down to rummage through a pile of papers on the floor. "You have to understand," he said as he rifled through the documents, "I have broader responsibilities than Alfred Adensnap. He was in charge of your British Museum's South American artifacts. I am in charge of this entire department. I deal with artifacts and architecture and art and . . . Ha!"

He stood up, clutching several sheets of yellowing parchment covered with Mayan hieroglyphs and Spanish handwriting. He carefully smoothed the pages out on the desk so that the friends could see. They all gathered around eagerly, even Dominique.

"I recognize that writing," said Emily at once. Emily, Ben, and Jack had all seen the handwriting before—on a manuscript in Adensnap's office. It was the hand of a sixteenth-century Spanish missionary who had worked among the descendants of the ancient Mayans. The friends knew he had written down the ritual that could banish Camazotz. Now it seemed he had collected a great deal more information besides.

Mayan hieroglyphs ran down the left side of the

parchment. The missionary had written in Spanish down the right. He had only managed a few lines before stopping. Perhaps he had been disturbed. Whatever the reason, he seemed never to have returned to it.

"So, you know of Sebastian Cabrillo, the missionary?" said the vicomte. He sounded pleased. "See what he says here—excuse me, I must translate from Spanish to French to English—'The four, being of great power and strength, when brought together would do great service to He Who Walks By Darkness.' And there it stops." The vicomte sighed. "I had always assumed it referred to four *people.* Four men, perhaps, four especially trusted servants of Camazotz. But look here." His finger traced a line of four glyphs—a bat, an eye, a crown, and a crescent moon. "I thought these might represent the four men. But perhaps they are actually pictures of the items in question. Of course, we don't know because no one can read the ancient Mayan." He looked up at Emily. "Or so I thought," he added.

Emily was already sitting down at the desk and pulling a pencil and paper toward her. She rummaged in her bag for her notebook and opened it on the desk. The vicomte looked on in astonishment.

"I'll translate it for you," Emily told him with a smile. "But I'm afraid you'll have to be patient."

Jack and Ben had been in this situation before. Waiting for Emily to translate a manuscript was singularly boring. The last time, Ben had taken Jack off to look around the British Museum. This time, the vicomte would not let them out of the office. All they could do was sit there and wait. The vicomte made them sit on a couch against one wall. It was a large couch, easily big enough for two boys and Dominique. So why, Jack wondered, did Dominique have to sit quite so close to him?

"You must have been so brave when you fought Camazotz in London, Jack," Dominique said. Her large eyes were shining as she took his hand and squeezed it. "You were a brave knight defending your city!"

"Well, Ben, too —" Jack started to say, but she wouldn't be interrupted.

"You were an English Joan of Arc," Dominique declared, "though Joan of Arc was a girl and you are not. She has always been my hero, but I think you are braver. She fought the English and not vampires. They had captured half of France and were still on the attack—the English, I mean, not the vampires. Oh, they are so frightening and I hate them all—I mean the vampires, not the English. . . ."

At least she isn't chattering about fashion, Jack thought.

At last Emily laid down her pen and sat back. Immediately the others gathered around her.

"Here is where you made your mistake," she said to the vicomte. "The missionary didn't understand this hieroglyph.

He thought the text said 'The four, being of great power and strength.' Really, it said 'The four, being *made by* great power and *endowing* strength.' Quite different."

Everyone was staring at the manuscript and Emily's notes as if they could understand them. Jack knew better than to try. He folded his arms and leaned against the wall next to the door.

"It is definitely four pieces, then?" asked the vicomte.

"Four pieces of an amulet, yes," replied Emily. "A bat, an eye, a crown, and a crescent moon. They were made to look distinct but also to fit together. The whole is far more powerful than the sum of its parts."

"What was the amulet for?" Ben inquired.

"A magical or a religious purpose, I would imagine," replied the vicomte.

"What, like Dominique's Chac talisman?" Jack asked.

"The same sort of thing," the vicomte agreed. "Does it say what the amulet would do, Emily?"

And it was at that moment that Jack realized he could feel a cold draft on the back of his head. He turned and saw that the door behind him had opened just a crack. He heard a floorboard creak and immediately grew suspicious. Was someone standing outside the office, eavesdropping?

"I haven't quite worked that out yet," Emily answered. "Camazotz really wanted it, though. The amulet was made to increase his power no end. I *think*—and this is very rough" — she ran her finger down a line of hieroglyphs — "I think Camazotz commanded one of his priests to fashion it, but the priest was a secret follower of Chac. He didn't dare disobey Camazotz, so he crafted the four pieces of the amulet, but he was reluctant to give them all to the vampire god because they would increase his power so much. He couldn't lie outright to Camazotz, but he could stall."

Jack casually straightened up and strolled away from the door. He wandered over to the room's second door. It was set between the bookshelves and led to the adjoining office. He tried the handle and found it wasn't locked.

The others were busy listening to Emily. "The priest decided to give the amulet to Camazotz one piece at a time," she was saying. "Camazotz only had the first piece when Chac's followers used the ritual of the blood rose on him and banished him to his cave. They tried to destroy the other pieces of the amulet, but they were too powerful to be destroyed by mere humans. So instead, the pieces were scattered around the empire."

Jack slipped into the neighboring office, which was empty. As he had hoped, there was another door that led back into the corridor. He left the door to the vicomte's office open so he could hear what was being said.

"And now Camazotz has two of the pieces," Ben remarked.

"Yes," said the vicomte. "I assume that the crown was the first piece he was given and that he took it with him to the cave, which is how he had it in London. Then he stole the bat statue, the second piece. The eye is the third piece. So where is the fourth?"

"He *might* have the fourth piece already," Ben pointed out anxiously.

"We must hope not," replied the vicomte.

Jack very slowly opened the door to the corridor and peered out. There was a boy by the door at the end of the corridor. He looked strangely familiar, and then Jack remembered that he had seen the lad in the gallery the day before, being chased off by a museum attendant.

Did the boy usually hang around the Louvre? Jack wondered. In which case, was it possible that he might know something about the attack on Professor Adensnap and the ransacking of the South American gallery? As Jack watched, he realized that the boy was certainly eavesdropping on Emily's conversation. He was a spy! Jack decided it was time to find out exactly how much the lad knew.

He took a stealthy step forward, but the shift in his weight made a floorboard creak under him. The boy spun around, startled. He let out a yell when he saw Jack, then took to his heels. But to escape, he had to run out of the corridor and that meant running straight past Jack.

Jack grabbed him by the scruff of his neck. The boy was small and light enough for Jack to stop him dead. "Oh, no, you don't!" he said.

The boy flailed his fists at him. Jack simply caught his wrists and held them. "I got some questions for you."

The boy writhed but he couldn't break Jack's grip. "Let go, English!" His voice was piping, and though he spoke to Jack in English, his French accent was strong.

"Why are you spying on us?" Jack demanded.

The boy stopped writhing. "I see something," he said slyly.

"Yeah?" Jack stared down at him. "Well, spit it out. What did you see?"

The boy peered shyly up at him. "Perhaps I see it with" — he grinned suddenly — "an *eye*?"

Jack was so surprised, he loosened his grip. Immediately the lad stamped hard on Jack's foot. Jack yelped and let go.

The boy fled. "You catch me first, English!" he shouted shrilly, laughing. Then he was out in the gallery.

"Why, you little . . ." Jack bellowed.

"Jack? What is happening?" He heard Dominique calling him, but he ignored her to run after the boy, who was now speeding past two surprised cleaners.

"Come and get me, English!" he taunted Jack over his shoulder. And that settled it. Any faint fondness Jack might have felt for him the day before evaporated. Now Jack just wanted to grab him and make him answer some questions.

The corridors of the Louvre flashed past as Jack's feet pounded on the polished floor. He caught momentary glimpses of angry or surprised visitors, but they quickly became a forgotten blur behind him. All his attention was focused on the small figure about fifty yards ahead of him.

The boy disappeared down a small side corridor. As Jack dove after him, he saw the lad vanish through a door at the end. Jack reached the door and hauled it open. He could hear the boy's footsteps echoing from a stone spiral staircase. So Jack pounded down the stairs after him and burst out into a narrow, unpainted stone passage. It was a far cry from the well-lit grandeur of the floors above. The boy was just disappearing around a corner at the end.

Jack paused when he reached that corner. Around the bend, the corridor was much darker. There were no windows here and all was in shadow. Jack could hear the receding footsteps still, but he wasn't going to run into prime vampire territory just like that.

But then daylight flooded the passageway. The boy had pulled open a door at the far end, and the noise of the city came pouring in along with the light. Jack looked down the length of the passage. There were no vampires, but for a moment the boy stood silhouetted in the doorway, looking back at Jack. Then he made a gesture that was rude in both French and English and ran off.

Jack followed him out onto the riverbank, the strip of land between the Louvre palace and the Seine. The boy was just standing there by the elegant iron span of the Pont des Arts. He stuck his thumbs in his ears and wiggled his fingers. But then he must have realized just how fast Jack was gaining on him, because he looked alarmed and fled. He turned suddenly and ran around the corner of the Louvre, away from the river.

Jack reached the corner just in time to see the boy reach the busy thoroughfare of the Rue de Rivoli. There were lots of people here—Parisians going about their daily business—but no one seemed interested in one boy chasing another.

To his surprise, Jack found he was breathing heavily. At the docks, he himself had fled more than once from an aggrieved victim and never felt the worse for it. Now he was struggling to keep up with a lad who was smaller and younger than he was. Living with the Coles had made him heavier and slower. Besides, his coat was thick and warm and he could feel himself starting to sweat with the effort of giving chase. But Jack still had his pride, and he actually enjoyed a good chase. He took a deep breath and set off again in pursuit, fumbling to undo his coat buttons and let the air in.

Finally he seemed to be gaining. The boy's defense consisted of getting away as quickly as possible—using up all his strength in one dash. Jack had tried that often before; it only worked if you could be sure your pursuer would give up before you did. And Jack had no intention of giving up.

The boy paused, panting, at the corner of a side street. He glanced back, saw Jack bearing down on him, and pelted into the small lane. Jack dodged around a fruit seller carrying a large basket of apples on his head and plunged into the side street.

He was immediately struck by the contrast between this small lane and the bustling Rue de Rivoli. Here, the buildings on either side were tall and rickety. They overhung the lane, almost blocking out the sky. An open sewer ditch ran down the middle of the road and Jack's feet splashed in filthy puddles. Washing lines on which tattered clothing had been optimistically hung out to dry were strung between the roofs.

The lane was much quieter than the road he had left, but there were still people here. They were the people Paris would rather forget—not a top hat or a fine dress among them. The city's poor sat about in the street, chatting. They watched the two lads run past with a bland indifference, or so Jack thought until an elderly woman casually put a leg out to hinder his pursuit. He managed to grind to a halt just before he tripped. "Hey, watch out!" he cried indignantly. The old woman puffed on a pipe and met his glare impassively.

Jack realized that the woman saw only his clothes and judged accordingly. He was a young lord here among the city's destitute population. These people saw him chasing a boy, one of their own, and decided to give the lad a helping hand. Jack would have done the same, once.

But where had the boy gone to now? Jack slowed to look up and down the lane. He groaned. There was no sign of the lad. Then "Can't catch me, English!" trilled a familiar voice, and Jack broke into a run again, though his legs and lungs ached and his heart pounded with the exercise.

The boy was poised to flee at the corner of a tiny alleyway. In fact, he was so obviously poised and waiting for Jack that a small warning bell sounded in Jack's head. He ignored it as the boy ran ahead of him up the alley. It was still daytime, there was still plenty of sunlight, and Jack felt confident he wasn't going to run into any vampires.

The alley narrowed. Even the boy had to dodge the obstacles here—barrels, piles of wood, a small cart. Jack was closing the gap. He could hear the boy's feet splashing in the mud and he saw the lad stagger slightly. Jack read the signs and knew he was going to catch the little ragamuffin at last.

The lane twisted this way and that until only Jack's keen sense of direction told him which way was what. The noise of the city center was muted now, muffled by the innumerable twists and turns behind him. More significant, Jack realized, was the fact that the sunlight was almost nonexistent here.

Too far, Jack, he told himself. *You're going too far into the shadows. If you don't catch him soon, just turn back. At least you'll have given the brat the fright of his life.*

The cobbled street gave way to a muddy track as Jack rounded another corner. This would be the last. If he didn't get the boy now, he decided he would have to give up.

He was just in time to see the boy dart into a hole in the wall. Jack slowed down as he approached the opening. It was a stone arch, low enough that he would have to stoop, but even in his current mood, Jack was not going to run into a dark hole in the ground where vampires could be lying in wait.

He squatted down on his haunches and peered inside. Just in front of him was the top of an iron ladder. That was all he could see in the darkness, but he could hear the receding patter of running feet splashing through water. As his eyes adjusted, he could make out the water itself, or at least the light glinting off the ripples. A gust of fetid air told him where he was. This was an entrance to the Paris sewers.

"Ha," Jack said out loud. "I don't think so." He turned away and bumped straight into a man standing behind him.

Jack had time to notice two things. The man was standing in shadows. And there seemed to be a red glow way back in the pupils of his eyes. Then, faster than Jack could move, the stranger reached out and shoved with both arms.

Jack staggered backward into the hole. The ground disappeared from under his feet and he felt himself tumbling into darkness.

Chapter Fourteen

Jack fell through the air with a yell and landed on a small platform next to the sewer's shallow stream. He gasped as he hit the bricks, but he was already scrambling to his feet. Dark shapes moved out of the shadows. Eyes gleamed red in pale faces. Vampires!

They were closing in on him. Jack dodged quickly. Groping fingers grabbed his coat, but he managed to wriggle away. He was at the bottom of the ladder, and the arch and sunlight were only six feet above him. Jack leapt for the rungs and quickly scrambled up the ladder. But before he could reach the top, strong hands grabbed him and pulled him back down. He lashed out with his feet. One of them hit something with a satisfying crunch. But more hands reached out to catch hold of him, and he was plucked off the ladder and thrown back onto the ground. Vampires surrounded him, pinning him down until he was completely unable to move.

"Aaagh!" Jack shouted. The cry echoed up and down the tunnel. It wasn't a scream of pain; it was a shout of anger and frustration with himself. He had walked right into a nest of vampires.

"We have not even begun to question you," said a voice in English. "Save your screams until later."

Jack still kicked and struggled as he was lifted up and carried farther down the tunnel, away from what little sunlight spilled through the archway. The vampires deposited him on another platform of damp brickwork, where he was spread-eagled as vampires held down his limbs. He looked around at them. They seemed a motley group of rich and poor. In Paris, as in London, Jack realized, Camazotz had recruited his army from all backgrounds.

A dark figure loomed over Jack. He wore a smart suit and looked very respectable, apart from his evil red eyes and the fangs protruding from his mouth. Strangely, Jack felt no fear, though he was certain he would soon be dead. He was still too exhilarated after the chase. But anger was a different matter—he felt plenty of that. "Shouldn't be surprised, finding you here in the sewers," he said. "It's where Camazotz belongs."

Some of the vampires holding him growled when he mentioned their master's name. The standing figure simply turned away and beckoned to someone. Jack heard approaching footsteps, and then the young boy was standing over him. Jack groaned again. The boy had been bait all the time. He had no doubt been sent to lure one of their party into the vampires' trap. And Jack had fallen for the trick. If he could have moved, he would have kicked himself.

The lad grinned impudently as the vampire gave him some coins. "May I have the coat, too?" he asked. "Winter is coming." He spoke French to the vampire, but Jack got the gist—especially when the vampire silently handed the lad Jack's coat. "Good-bye, English!" the boy sang out before scampering off into the darkness.

Despite everything, Jack suddenly felt sorry for the lad. If a stranger had come up to him in London when he had been living on the streets and offered him money to get himself chased, he would have done exactly the same thing. The boy couldn't know the kind of creature he was working for. Jack hoped he would never have cause to find out.

"And now," the vampire said, turning back to Jack and thoughtfully speaking in English, "you know what we want."

Jack glared at him. "A bath?" he suggested.

The vampire didn't smile. He held up one finger and slowly put it against Jack's shoulder. Jack squinted down at it and saw the finger shift and blur into a claw. He drew in his breath sharply as the tip punctured his skin. It stung unbearably. Jack guessed that more pain was to come.

"Your friend the vicomte has property belonging to the master," said the vampire. "Where is it?"

"Get lost," Jack gasped.

Then the vampire drove his claw deep into Jack's shoulder and twisted it. Jack convulsed and screamed in pain. His cries echoed down the dank tunnel. The vampire pulled his claw out, and Jack felt blood running down his shoulder beneath his torn shirt.

"Why do we not just turn him?" asked one of the vampires holding him. "Then all his knowledge will be ours."

"The master forbade it. Do not question the master," the leader snapped. "Besides . . ." He grinned. "This is more entertaining. And we may yet feed on him."

Jack looked at the approaching claw with wide eyes. His shoulder throbbed as if a white-hot poker had been burned into it. "You want entertaining?" he croaked. "I'll entertain you."

The claw stopped.

"In London," Jack said, "we made this potion against Camazotz. . . ."

Another growl came from the vampires, and their leader rested his claw lightly against the wound in Jack's shoulder, ready for another thrust. Jack began to speak more quickly, his voice rising higher with fear. If they were going to hurt him, he had decided he would hurt them back in the only way he could, by insulting their master.

"And we used it to banish him. And he screamed, all girly-like, and then ran away down to Hell and —" The claw pricked his skin and Jack couldn't go on. He clenched his teeth, squeezed his eyes shut, and waited for the next thrust of agony.

It didn't come. Jack opened his eyes slowly, one at a time, and saw the vampire straightening up. His claws had become hands again.

"Bring him," he commanded.

Rough hands picked Jack up and carried him off into the darkness. The farther they went, the more Jack thought that the sewers seemed like the ideal home for the servants of Camazotz. Sprawling beneath the streets and houses, the sewers had entrances and exits in every part of the city. Jack tried to keep track of the route they were taking, but it twisted and turned so much that he completely lost his way. In the faint light that filtered down from the surface through vents and grilles, Jack saw pitfalls in places where the floor had collapsed, but the light was too scant for him to make out much else in the mist and murk.

He racked his brains for everything he could remember about Camazotz—in particular, for every failure and every humiliation the demon god had suffered at the hands of Ben and Emily and himself. If the vampires started torturing him again, Jack was determined to blurt out all those memories before he told the vampires anything useful.

The vampire party came to a halt. Lanterns flickered on the walls, their flames threatening to die in the poisonous air, but by their choked illumination Jack could see that he was now in a wider chamber. Several dark, narrow tunnels led off in different directions. The brick walls were dripping with slime.

A row of wooden doors ran along one wall of the chamber, with metal grilles set into the rotten wood. They looked like dungeon cells. A vampire pulled the nearest door open and threw Jack inside. He hit the stone floor, landing in what felt like about three feet of slime. He scrambled quickly to his feet. He suspected that the cells flooded whenever the water level in the sewers rose, and he didn't want to be close to whatever was down there in the dark, by his feet.

The door was slammed shut and he heard the bolt being thrown. Then the little light that came through the grille was momentarily obscured by the head of the suited vampire. "The kings of France used this place to keep prisoners out of sight," he said dryly. "They will not object if we follow suit. Now we will consult with the master."

He turned away, and Jack hurried across the cell to peer through the grille. He was just in time to see the last of his captors transform into a bat and fly off down a tunnel. He was alone in the darkness.

He leaned against the back wall of the cell. He couldn't see if there was any kind of bench or bed, but knowing what covered the floor, he wanted to stay on his feet—especially since he also had an open wound he needed to keep as clean as he could.

His shoulder ached abominably, particularly when he let his arm hang, so he cradled his bad arm with his good one and waited. The dark silence of the sewers seemed to close in around him. He was completely cut off from the noise and bustle of the city above. He realized that no one knew where he was. The vampires could just forget about him, and he would starve to death. His bones would lie here, never to be found.

"Cheer up, Jack," he said out loud, just to hear a human voice. "You been in worse than this." He paused a moment. "No, you ain't," he admitted. "Forget I said that."

Outside the cell there was a brief squeak and some scampering. He froze, then realized it was only rats.

"Camazotz," he said, just to hear the word—and because the vampires had been angry when he said it earlier. Then, again, "Camazotz." *Put them together and they make a kind of chant*, he thought. *What rhymed with Camazotz?*

"He's stupider than a pile of pots," he said, and grinned to himself in the darkness.

Footsteps sounded outside, splashing through the slime. Jack groaned. It seemed the vampires were back already.

"Jack! Are you in there?" came a soft voice in the gloom. And, to his surprise and delight, Jack saw Dominique's face at the grille.

Chapter Fifteen

“Dominique!” Jack exclaimed. He scrambled across the cell to the door. “How did you get here?”

“I have been following you since you ran out of the office!” she told him. “Everyone else was busy with the translation, but I saw you leave, and I followed. I was just in time to see you run off, so I ran after you. I tried to keep up, but you are a faster runner—and I have to wear this long dress, which is not practical for running, even though it was brand-new this season. It replaces a dress I have had since I was eleven. It has a frilled hemline and three over-laid layers—I mean the old dress, not this one. This has no pleats, which is perhaps a *little* old-fashioned, but as you can see, the hemline is quite straight and that is much more popular this year. . . .”

Jack shut his eyes. “So you ran all the way from the Louvre to talk about this year’s fashions?” he said.

“Oh!” Dominique suddenly seemed to remember where she was. “Well, several times I lost sight of you alto-gether, but I asked some passersby if they had seen a running boy. They said you had gone into the sewer and I followed. Oh, Jack! I heard a terrible, terrible scream!"

"Uh, yeah," Jack admitted. "That were me."

"Did they hurt you, Jack?" Dominique asked breathlessly.

"No, we was just seeing who could sing the loudest," he snapped. "Of *course* they —" He broke off as he saw her face crumple.

"Oh, Jack, I know you do not like me," she said sadly. "But I try to be brave like you . . . and it is very dark down here . . . and I followed you, though I was terrified, and my skirt is ruined . . . and the mice are very, *very* big down here . . . and . . ."

Jack groaned and cursed himself for his unkindness. "Dominique," he said, "you . . ." He paused again as he realized that, to his surprise, what he was about to say was absolutely true. "You been a great friend and I *do* like you." She was warm and human and alive, she was down here in this terrible, stinking place, and she had come for him. Yes, Jack liked her. "And I'm sorry I been rude to you," he added.

Dominique's eyes shone. "Oh, Jack, how can I get you out?"

"I think there's a bolt," he said.

"Oh, yes. It is high up." Dominique stretched up and, with effort, managed to pull the bolt back.

Jack pushed the door open and stepped out of the cell.

Dominique threw her arms around him. "You are free!" she cried happily.

"Aagh!" Jack groaned as pain lanced through his shoulder.

Dominique quickly let him go. "Did I hurt you?"

"No, you . . ." He was about to be sarcastic again but thought better of it. "No," he said. "Come on. We need to find a way out."

They looked around the chamber at the passages that led off in all directions.

"The vampires went that way," Jack said, pointing to one of them.

"I came along this one," Dominique put in, indicating another. But then she paused. "I think."

Jack had to admit that they all looked alike. In fact, he wasn't entirely sure which one the vampires had taken. He and Dominique were stuck in a labyrinth of sewers, with no idea how to get out.

But the labyrinth provided a clue—the floor sloped. Follow the slope downward, Jack reasoned, and you must come to the river. He bent down to peer at the trickle of water running past his feet. "If we go back to the river, we go back to the Louvre," he said, and he led Dominique into a tunnel.

They walked straight into utter blackness. The chamber had been dimly lit by lanterns, but the tunnels were not. Jack could see nothing, but he could feel solid ground beneath his feet, and when he stretched out his one good arm to the side, he felt the wall. Cautiously he edged one foot forward, fearing a pitfall, but the floor seemed to continue smoothly, so he carefully advanced into the passage, with Dominique following.

He tried to make the most of the little information his senses could provide. Touch guided him along the slimy walls of the sewer. Sight showed the faint patches of light that indicated possible exits. And most important of all, Jack knew that his hearing would be his earliest warning that the vampires were coming.

A hollow roar echoed down the passage, making Jack jump. Dominique squeaked. For a moment they clung to each other, listening hard for any further sounds and waiting for their pounding hearts to calm down.

Another roar.

"Just water," Jack decided. "Come on."

They moved onward, into the darkness. After some minutes of this slow progress, their eyes adjusted to the dim light from the vent holes high above and they were able to move faster. The slimy floor offered little grip, and they slipped and staggered as they hurried along, but Jack was sure they were heading in the right direction. He was hot and thirsty, but although water streamed and trickled all around him, there was none to drink. From time to time he was revived by a faint gust of fresh air from a vent, but that was all.

Before long, the two friends found themselves at a junction. They could turn left or right, but it was too dark to see which way the water was flowing. Jack took a few steps in one direction, then the other, trying to gauge the slope of the floor. "I think this is —" he began, and then a terrible cry echoed down the tunnel behind them. The vampires had discovered Jack's absence.

"Come on!" Jack said. He grabbed Dominique's hand and they ran to the left, not knowing where it would lead them, but desperate to put as much distance as possible between themselves and the vampires.

They splashed and scrambled madly along the passage as quickly as they could go. And then Jack heard a faint screeching sound that he recognized with a thrill of horror. "They've changed into bats," he told Dominique, and shuddered, remembering how Camazotz's bats had hunted him and his friends through the dark alleys of Soho. *Down here*, he thought grimly, *the vampires were really in their element.* They didn't need to see to know where they were going, and in flight, the bats were incredibly swift and agile, able to change direction in the blink of an eye.

"Bats?" Dominique queried.

"They're still vampires," Jack explained. "Hurry."

They staggered on, praying they could keep ahead of the bats long enough to find an exit to the sunlit world outside.

Jack gasped suddenly and turned to look behind him. There wasn't anything there, but he could have sworn he had felt something.

"Jack?" Dominique queried breathlessly.

"Nothing," he muttered. "Come on." He turned back and immediately sensed it again—an unpleasant feeling, like being watched by somebody or *something*. And suddenly he realized what it was. The bats were flying and hunting by echolocation, and when they came close enough, Jack could feel it. Perhaps it was something to do with being in such an enclosed space, but Jack didn't stop to analyze it further.

He looked around desperately and spotted an alcove in the wall ahead. Without a second thought, Jack dragged Dominique over to it and pulled her inside, clapping his hand over her mouth to muffle her startled scream. Seconds later two dark shapes swept by, almost grazing Jack with the tips of their wings.

Jack waited a good minute before letting Dominique go.

"How did you know?" she whispered, wide-eyed and terrified.

"I felt them," Jack said. "It's how they hunt. They use noise to find their victims. It's not *loud* noise but somehow I could sort of feel it." He peered down the passageway, the way the vampires had gone. "We should try another way." He took Dominique by the hand and they carried on blindly into the darkness.

The idea of following the flow of the water didn't work anymore. They were away from the main stream now and Jack had no idea where they were heading. Up, down, left, right . . . it all became meaningless in this dark, tangled underworld.

Could they possibly find a way out before the vampires found them? Jack wondered. He really didn't think so. They were completely lost, surrounded by vampires, and practically blinded by darkness. *It's only a matter of time before they track us down*, he thought, but he didn't want to scare Dominique, so he said nothing and forged ahead as quickly and quietly as possible.

And then he remembered something that might just give them a chance against the vampire horde. "Hey," he whispered, "did you bring your tal—"

"Look!" Dominique exclaimed suddenly. "Light!"

The light ahead was very dim, but it *did* look like daylight. They ran forward eagerly and found themselves in another chamber—circular and domed. Other passages led out of it. The daylight was coming from a small grating in the pinnacle of the dome above. One faint sunbeam shone straight down into the gloomy sewers. Jack and Dominique stood underneath it, squinting up.

"Much too high," Jack muttered sadly.

That strange feeling of being watched suddenly came to him again. This time it was overwhelming. "Duck!" he yelled, and dropped to the grimy floor, pulling Dominique down with him. A pair of bats swooped ahead, screeching in fury at having missed their targets.

The bats circled around the chamber and then headed back toward the two friends. Jack gazed around desperately, looking for some sort of weapon or any means of escape. He glanced at the sunbeam in the middle of the room. The sunlight offered some protection, but the beam was so thin—there would only be room for one person to stand in it. "Dominique!" he cried. "Stand in the sun—"

But Dominique was standing, tall and determined, confronting the bats.

"No!" Jack shouted in horror. "Get out of the way!"

The bats flew down at the little French girl, their vicious claws extended and their fangs gleaming ominously in the faint daylight. At the very last moment, Dominique held out her talisman. The bats screamed in fury and veered away.

Jack sighed with relief, though his heart was still pounding. "I wish you wouldn't do that," he muttered.

The bats were circling the chamber now, always keeping a safe distance from Dominique's talisman. Jack and Dominique took advantage of this to edge their way over to the downhill tunnel. Then they plunged back into the darkness of the passageways.

A high squeal from the vampires behind them set Jack's teeth on edge. It didn't draw any closer, which meant the vampires weren't following, but it filled the air around them and rang painfully in Jack's head. Another, similar squeal came out of a side tunnel, shortly followed by more screeches from every direction. The cries echoed through the labyrinth. The sound was like nails scraping on slate, and Jack shuddered.

Only one direction radiated silence, and that was the one they had to take. Jack realized that he and Dominique were being herded, propelled by walls of sound that welled out of the darkness on all sides. And if they were being herded, that meant there was a trap ahead. But they had no choice. They couldn't go back and they couldn't stay where they were. "Be ready," Jack whispered nervously.

Dominique simply nodded, her face a pale blur in the darkness, and they stumbled on together.

The screeching stopped so suddenly that Jack's ears continued to ring. He and Dominique had come to another round subterranean chamber. They looked at each other, uncertain what to expect. Then Dominique took a firm hold of her talisman and the two of them stepped cautiously forward.

Bats swooped down from the ceiling and circled around them. Three of them hovered briefly in midair before Jack and Dominique. Then their outlines changed and they dropped to the ground, straightening up as men. One of them was the leader who had tortured Jack. "You cannot escape," he hissed. "We will prevent it."

"Yeah?" Jack demanded. He forced himself to sound confident, though he had never felt less so. "Then come and get us," he said bravely.

The vampire took one step forward, then recoiled as Dominique's talisman took effect.

"It's been fun," Jack said, heartened by the talisman's influence. "But frankly the accommodation weren't up to scratch, so we'll take our business elsewhere, if you don't mind."

The vampire hissed angrily in response but didn't move.

"Come on," Jack muttered to Dominique, and they ran into the only passage that led out of the chamber. More vampires in human form loomed ahead of them, but they, too, recoiled from Dominique. They backed away down the passage as she advanced. Behind the friends, other vampires were starting to follow, venturing as close as they could to the talisman of Chac.

"You are so brave, Jack," Dominique said quietly. "I hope I can be like you."

"I hope you don't need to —" Jack began.

He stopped as Dominique gasped in despair. The tunnel had widened out again into a chamber, and Jack immediately realized what his companion had seen. The chamber was a dead end. They were at the bottom of a circular pit, and the only way out was via an old, rusted ladder that led up to the next level.

There were vampires ahead of them, spread out around the edges of the pit. Jack and Dominique peered up into the darkness at the top of the ladder. Another tunnel seemed to lead away from it and more dark figures waited up there, their eyes glowing red in the darkness.

"Jack, we cannot climb the ladder together," Dominique whispered miserably.

Jack looked at the ladder. She was right. It was narrow and almost rusted through. He was not sure it would bear the weight of one of them, let alone both. If they were to go up it at all, it would have to be one at a time. And there was only one talisman.

Jack closed his eyes and, with an immense effort of will, pushed away the feeling of despair that threatened to overwhelm him. Then he opened his eyes again. "You go up the ladder," he said to Dominique. "Wave the talisman at the vampires up there. They won't be able to touch you. Then go and tell the others what has happened."

Dominique's eyes filled with tears. "No, Jack, no! I can't leave you here!"

"You have to!" Jack insisted. "You wanted to be brave. . . ."

He glanced at the vampires. They had made the same assessment he had and were grinning at him. A mass of white fangs gleamed in the darkness. "Look," he said, more quietly and urgently. "They didn't kill me before. They won't now." He *hoped* that was true, but they had gone to consult with the master, and who knew what Camazotz had said? Jack was fairly sure he was going to die, but he was determined not to let Dominique know that. "Please, Dominique, for me. Go now, please?"

She began to sob. "Jack . . ." she moaned. But she turned to the ladder and began to climb. Then she turned back and moved to fling her arms around him one last time before she remembered his injury and drew back.

Instead, Jack put his arms around her and hugged her and held her tight for a moment. She kissed him quickly on both cheeks and he kissed her once on the forehead. All he could think of was that she was warm and alive, and he might never feel someone warm and alive again. Indeed, he might very soon be cold and dead himself.

Jack slowly released Dominique and pushed her gently toward the ladder. She started to climb, and the vampires at the top drew back sharply as she approached. When she reached the top, she stopped and looked down at Jack. "We'll be back to rescue you, Jack!" she promised in a choked voice, and then she disappeared from view.

Jack turned back to the advancing horde of vampires. He had seen bodies dragged out of the Thames. Would his own corpse turn up in the Seine in a few days' time, drained and lifeless? Well, if he had to die, then he was determined to be brave and defiant to the last. And if he made them angry, he reasoned, they might at least do it quickly.

"All together now," he said, and his voice only trembled slightly. "One, two, three. Camazotz, Camazotz, he's stupider —"

His voice was cut off in a cry of pain as the vampires overwhelmed him.

Chapter Sixteen

Emily looked up from her work in surprise as Dominique burst into the office. The vicomte had been stacking the scattered documents in piles, while Emily worked on the translation and Ben fretted. Dominique stumbled against one of the piles and sent the papers flying again.

If the vicomte had been about to scold her, he stopped when he saw the state she was in. "Dominique! Why have you been so long? And what has happened to you?"

Emily could scarcely believe her eyes. Dominique's once immaculate clothes were soaked and stained. Her face was flushed and her hair was tumbling wildly down around her face. She also smelled horribly of the Paris sewers.

"Uncle Henri, they have Jack, the monsters have taken him!" Dominique declared.

Ben and Emily leapt to their feet.

"They have him?" Ben cried, aghast. "Jack's . . . dead?"

"No, no!" Dominique said hastily. "At least, I do not think . . . but . . . and they . . ."

Emily made Dominique sit down and take some deep breaths. The vicomte, usually so assured, seemed at a loss to know how to deal with his distressed niece. Emily asked him to go get Dominique a drink of water. Then Dominique told her story.

She had gotten to the entrance of the sewers, when she had heard the sounds of a scuffle, and then receding footsteps as the vampires carried Jack away. Clutching her talisman, Dominique had forced herself to climb down into the darkness and follow. When she heard Jack scream, she had almost turned and run back to the sunlight, but she had kept going and managed to free Jack from his cell.

Finally she described their miserable journey back through the labyrinth of tunnels and how they had been forced to separate. There had been no more dead ends. Her talisman had gotten her through the remaining vampires and she had climbed up through a drain in the Champs Elysées. From there she had run all the way back to the Louvre.

"I . . . I heard him scream again," Dominique said. She swallowed hard, clearly struggling not to cry. "So, perhaps . . ."

Emily put her arms around her.

"No," the vicomte assured her. "I am certain Jack is still alive. They went to a lot of trouble to catch him, and I can think of a very good reason why they might spare him, for the time being, at least."

"He's a hostage," Ben said quietly. "Camazotz wants the eye."

"That would be my guess," the vicomte agreed. He

looked out the window. The sun was low on the horizon, and the Paris shadows were lengthening. "Camazotz will send his emissary shortly, assuming he has ransom in mind," the vicomte said. But then he stood up decisively and picked up his hat. "But the great Napoleon never won a battle by sitting and waiting. You must always take the fight to the enemy. Dominique, show us to this sewer!"

Dominique led them to the small hole in the wall where Jack had been abducted. "This is it," she said quietly.

The vicomte crouched down on the muddy cobbles and peered into the darkness, much as Jack had done. "Well . . ." he began.

"Look, sir," Ben said suddenly in a low, tense voice.

The vicomte glanced up, then slowly got to his feet. The sun was well below the rooftops of Paris, and black shapes fluttered down from the dark sky. The four humans drew closer together instinctively as the bats flew over them.

"Dominique!" said the vicomte, and she quickly held the talisman up for the vampires to see. The bats veered abruptly away, their eyes flashing angrily. They split into two groups. One landed up the lane from the humans; the other settled between the friends and the Rue de Rivoli. The four companions were trapped.

The bats shifted into their human forms. Emily, Ben, and Dominique had seen it before, but the vicomte gasped as the bats seemed to swell and blur, suddenly becoming human.

Now the friends stood between two groups of men and women. Ben noticed gentlemen and beggars, ladies of society and fishwives from the market. They were all united in service to their master.

"*Monsieur le vicomte,*" said a man in a suit, stepping forward. He was tall and pale, his eyes a red gleam below the rim of his top hat. Dominique held the talisman up again, and the man flinched. "Please, there is no need for that," he said, reverting to English. Ben assumed that this was for the benefit of himself and Emily.

"May I help you?" asked the vicomte with icy courtesy.

"I have a message from the master concerning the English boy," said the vampire.

"And that is?"

"You are to take the master's property to the Père-Lachaise Cemetery at midnight tonight. There you will exchange it for your young friend."

"A cemetery," remarked the vicomte. "How appropriate!"

The man held up his hands. "Please, I simply deliver the message. You can take it or leave it."

"We do not know that Jack is alive!" Dominique put in anxiously.

The vampire smiled. "Would you like one of his hands freshly severed, to show he was alive when we took it? It can be arranged," he said nastily.

Dominique went pale, and the vicomte put a gentle hand on her shoulder. "We will consider the exchange you propose," he said.

The vampire touched a finger to his hat in an ironic salute, then barked, "*Partons!*" Immediately the vampires leapt into the air, changing into bats and flying off into the night.

Dominique, Ben, and Emily all opened their mouths to speak, but the vicomte held up a hand to silence them. "We will discuss this quandary when we are safely back at my office," he said firmly.

Chapter Seventeen

The vicomte said only one thing as they walked back to the Louvre. "We cannot give up the eye. It is as simple as that." He would not entertain further discussion until they were back in the museum.

"Benedict, please check the other room," the vicomte said as they entered his office. He drew the curtains while Ben opened the connecting door and peered into the adjoining room.

"There's no one there," he reported.

"Good." The vicomte shut the main door and stood with his back to it. "We are alone. Now we can make plans."

"We must rescue Jack, sir, and we must do it as soon as possible," Ben began.

"But Camazotz holds all the cards," said the vicomte. "He *knows* where Jack is, while we could never hope to find him in this city. The simplest way to save Jack is to part with the eye—but that is out of the question."

"Why?" Ben demanded.

"Oh, Uncle Henri!" Dominique exclaimed at the same time.

"*Enough!*" the vicomte bellowed. "A brave and noble heart beats inside that young man," he said more calmly, "and long may it continue to do so. But there are many millions of brave and noble hearts in this world of ours, and if Camazotz gains the amulet, they will all be at risk. Can we allow that to happen?"

"But we don't even know what the amulet does, sir!" Ben pointed out.

"No, we do not," the vicomte agreed. "However, Camazotz has gone to great lengths to acquire the pieces. He is not merely looking for a souvenir of the old days. Whatever it does, it will give him powers even greater than those he has now. Hundreds of thousands died in the days of the Maya, and back then Camazotz had no amulet. We cannot afford to let him grow yet more powerful. Think about it—would Jack himself want to live in a world where he had been saved at the cost of everyone else? Would he be grateful?" He looked at Ben. "Well?"

Ben could barely meet his eyes. "No, sir," he whispered. "But . . ."

"I hate the thought of sacrificing your friend every bit as much as you do," the vicomte sighed. "But if it is Jack or the amulet —"

"One *quarter* of the amulet, Uncle Henri," Dominique put in.

The vicomte looked at her. "And it will mean Camazotz then has *three* quarters!" he said. "He will need only one more piece to complete the amulet."

"Then we'll just have to make sure we find the fourth piece first," Ben declared. With the death of Professor Adensnap, he had lost a good and valued friend, and he didn't think he could bear to lose another. "From what we know, it's almost certainly still in Mexico. You would know if such an artifact had been discovered. Sir, you're a rich and powerful man. If anyone can help find the fourth piece, it is you."

The vicomte shook his head sadly. "It is kind of you to say so, my friend, but you need not resort to flattery. It will not change my mind. I must consider what is best for the world at large, unfortunately, and not what is best for our young friend Jack."

Dominique went over and put her arms around her uncle. Ben had a horrible feeling she was going to resort to wheedling. But he was wrong.

"Dear Uncle Henri, Jack has risked his life for me. He is only with the monsters now because he put my freedom ahead of his own. He could easily have taken my talisman and saved himself, but he did not."

"I know, my dear, there is no doubting Jack's courage, but we must consider what is at risk —"

"Sir," Emily interrupted, surprising everybody. She had listened in silence as the argument raged. Now she stood, calm and dignified, in the center of the room. The others turned to stare at her. "You asked if we should sacrifice the world to save Jack," she continued. "But I ask, can we now leave Jack to die, when we know we have the means to save him? To give Camazotz this one piece of the amulet will not necessarily condemn the world, but to withhold it will certainly condemn Jack."

There was something indefinably compelling about Emily's words. Perhaps it was the calmness in her voice or the steadiness of her gaze. *Whatever it was*, Ben thought, *it had made the vicomte falter for the first time.*

All of them waited for the Frenchman's response. Eventually he bowed to Emily and said, "You are right, mademoiselle. Your friend saved my niece at the risk of his own life, and for that I am forever in his debt. While there is still a chance we may prevent Camazotz from gaining the fourth and final piece of the amulet, we cannot, in all conscience, sacrifice this young man."

"Oh, Uncle Henri!" Dominique sighed with relief.

"So it's agreed," Ben said solemnly. "We will work together to find the fourth piece of the amulet and keep it from Camazotz. But first—tonight—we take the eye to the cemetery and rescue Jack!"

Chapter Eighteen

"Sir, I *have* to do it!" Ben insisted.

The vicomte's coach rattled through the dark streets. The four passengers swayed gently in their seats.

But there was nothing gentle about the argument that had started on the way back to the vicomte's house. It had continued while Dominique took a bath and changed her clothes—to remove the smell of the sewers. And it still raged now, as the coach carried them swiftly through the night to the Père-Lachaise Cemetery.

The vicomte had agreed that they should rescue Jack. He had even reluctantly agreed that Dominique could come, too, provided she wore her talisman. But he would not agree to let Ben hand over the eye. "No, Benedict," he said firmly. "For the last time, you are still a boy. What kind of man would I be to send you into danger like this?"

"I've been in danger before!" Ben argued.

"No doubt, but that was unavoidable. I will not let you risk your life to do something that I can do myself. I have inherited responsibility for you from poor Alfred, and that is that."

The vicomte patted the pocket of his coat where he kept the eye.

"Sir," Ben tried one last time. "If . . ."

"If you want it, Benedict, you will have to wrestle it from me," the vicomte said, with the ghost of a smile. "And that would be most undignified."

Ben lapsed into a dour silence.

The cemetery of Père-Lachaise was on a small hill to the east of Paris. The coach pulled up at the gates shortly before midnight. The four climbed out and looked around. In one direction, they could see the bright lights of the crowded city. In the other, they saw nothing but gravestones and darkness.

Their breath formed clouds in the cold air as they peered through the gates. They shivered, though they were wrapped up warmly against the cold. Emily, Ben, and Dominique had thick woolen coats and caps. The vicomte wore an elegant velvet coat, a silk scarf, and a top hat.

He drew the eye out of his pocket and looked at it. "All is ready," he said. He glanced at Ben. "I am sorry, Benedict, but I do insist."

Ben sighed and nodded. "Yes, sir." Suddenly he frowned and leaned forward, staring at the amulet in the vicomte's hand. "What's that?" he asked, and took the eye from the Frenchman's unsuspecting grasp. He studied it closely, then slipped it into his own pocket. "Oh, it's nothing," he said casually, and started to walk toward the gates. "My mistake."

"Benedict!" the vicomte exclaimed. "We agreed . . ."

Ben turned back. "No, sir," he said, looking determined. "With respect, *you* agreed. But now I am telling you *I* will hand over the eye. It's no more than Jack would do in my place. In fact, if Jack had never met me, he wouldn't be in danger now. This is *my* job."

Emily quickly moved to stand between Ben and the vicomte. "Sir," she said gently, "if you want to get the eye from Ben, I think you'll have to wrestle it from him."

"And that would be most undignified," Dominique added firmly.

The vicomte stared at all three of them, but then he threw his hands up in the air. "Perverse children. But very well. I am French. We understand such gestures." He turned to his coachman. "Wait here," he instructed, though the driver needed no telling. Then he held up an oil lamp to light their way, and they set off through the gates.

A long driveway led them up the hill. It was bordered by tall, dark trees. The clouds broke and a full moon shone down upon them. Still, they had to watch their feet. The ground was uneven and there was not quite enough light to show the potholes.

They walked slowly and steadily, Dominique clutching her talisman. The night air was cool and damp and seemed to soak up all sound. Ben and Emily walked in front, peering into the trees on either side for signs of movement—and, in particular, any gleaming red eyes. All they saw were tombs and monuments. The cemetery was a fantastic jumble of religious carvings and shapes, ghostly and deserted in the moonlight.

They reached the top of the hill, and a cloud of mist suddenly drifted out of nowhere. The vicomte crossed himself nervously. The vapor wrapped itself around them and shimmered with a pearly light that gave off no warmth.

Then Camazotz spoke out of the mist. "*Stop!*"

Ben recognized the voice of the vampire god, and he knew Emily would, too. It came from no human throat and from no fixed point, either. It simply echoed out of the air around them. The words sounded guttural and harsh and seemed to vibrate in their bones.

"*I see you have brought the toy that my servants cannot approach. What for? Are you losing your courage,* boy*?*" Camazotz said the last word with audible fury. Ben suddenly remembered Professor Adensnap explaining to him just how passionately Camazotz must hate him, because every time Ben had gone up against the Mayan god, against all likelihood and reason, Camazotz had lost.

"Do—" the vicomte started to say, but his voice disappeared in a dry whisper. He swallowed and tried again. "Do you have our friend, monsieur?"

A ghastly chuckle came out of the fog. "*Perhaps. But you are hardly in a position to make demands.*"

"Oh, I think we are." Ben stepped forward and held up

the eye. "Because you don't get *this* until we know Jack's alive and well."

There was a pause, and then Jack's voice called out of the mist. "Ben? Emily?"

"We're here, Jack," Emily shouted back.

"He could be one of them by now," the vicomte murmured.

"I know, sir," Ben replied. "Jack, it's Ben. How did they catch you?"

"How did they catch me?" There was no mistaking the disgust in Jack's voice. "Only conned me, didn't they? And then —" His voice broke off suddenly in a gasp of pain.

Camazotz spoke again. "*Enough. Bring me the eye.*"

"Be careful, Ben," Emily whispered. Ben bit his lip, squared his shoulders, and took a step forward.

An icy gust of wind struck his face and almost blew him off his feet.

"*Not you,* boy." Again, they could all hear the hatred. "*I* will *have dealings with you, but now is not the time. Montargis, come to me.*"

Ben and the vicomte locked gazes, and then Ben slowly handed over the eye.

"It seems I am to be a hero after all," the vicomte said with a brave smile.

"Uncle Henri!" Dominique said anxiously, her eyes filling with tears.

Her uncle patted her on the cheek. "Have a brave heart,

Dominique," he whispered. Then he crossed himself and took a deep breath.

Ben, Emily, and Dominique watched the vicomte step forward, holding the eye in front of him, until he was swallowed up in the mist.

Chapter Nineteen

Blood pounded in Ben's ears and his chest felt tight. He suddenly realized he hadn't taken a breath since the vicomte vanished. He made himself breathe in, then breathe out again. He stared into the fog, willing it to clear.

Then the mist swirled and dark figures appeared, walking toward the friends. Soon, Ben could see that they were the vicomte and Jack. Jack was coatless and blindfolded, his hands tied behind his back. His clothes were filthy from his time in the sewers, and his shirt was stained with blood. The vicomte was guiding him with one hand.

"Jack!" Dominique exclaimed in delight. Jack looked around blindly, trying to work out where she was.

"Yes, it is him," said the vicomte, and he turned back to look at the mist. It was dissolving as rapidly as it had come. "That was an experience I really do not wish to repeat."

"Turn around, Jack," said Emily, reaching to undo the knot of his blindfold. Meanwhile Ben was setting his hands free.

Jack turned around, wringing his wrists to get the blood

circulating again. There was a big grin on his face. "Evenin', all," he said.

"Oh, Jack, I'm so glad," said Dominique, and she hugged him—gently—which seemed to please him.

"Good to see you, too, Dominique," he replied.

"It's good to have you back," Emily said with a soft smile, and Jack grinned at her.

Ben borrowed Dominique's talisman. "Here, Jack, catch," he called, and threw the pendant through the air.

Jack caught it with his good hand, looked at it, and grinned again. "Very pretty," he said, tossing it back to Ben. "But it don't go with my eyes."

Ben finally allowed himself to relax. He laughed as he handed the talisman back to Dominique. "It's great to see you, Jack."

"Don't blame you for checking, mate," Jack told him.

"Jack, you're hurt," Emily realized with concern.

"Yeah." Jack flexed his shoulder and winced. "It's still sore—but it feels better than it did. They stuck a claw in me, trying to make me talk. I thought they was going to do a lot worse, but no. Apparently Camazotz is saving me for something else!"

"Well, you're safe now," said Emily.

"We brought a change of clothes along for you, Jack," Ben told him. "You can change in the coach. No offense, but you smell terrible."

"What, me?" Jack pretended to be outraged. "This is the new scent for gentlemen, this is."

"I think we have delayed long enough," the vicomte said. He looked back to where the mist had been. It had cleared completely now, and there was no sign of Camazotz or his vampires. "Where did the vampires go?"

"They probably turned into bats and flew off," Ben replied. "But you're right, sir, we should go."

They set off gratefully back down the hill, still glancing nervously from side to side, in case the vampires had an unpleasant surprise planned. Astonishingly Camazotz seemed to have kept his word.

"But why should he not?" Dominique said when Ben expressed surprise at this. "He has what he wants."

"Yes, he does," Ben agreed. He shuddered. "But I'm quite sure he still has something terrible planned for all of us."

Chapter Twenty

They let Jack change inside the coach, then climbed in after him.

"The museum," the vicomte instructed the driver. Jack looked at him in surprise as the coach moved off. "We need the parchment that Emily has been translating, and we need her notes," the Frenchman explained. "In fact, I want to gather up every parchment that might conceivably be of help to Camazotz and get them into the security of a private home as soon as possible."

"He might already be at the museum, sir," Ben pointed out. "He can fly, after all."

The vicomte smiled. "Even if he is, we have Dominique's marvelous talisman to protect us."

The plan made sense, and Jack could see the importance of retrieving the documents, but still he peered nervously out the windows as they reached the Place du Carrousel in front of the Louvre. The museum loomed darkly against the night sky, only lit from within by the occasional lamp in an office or gallery.

They drew up at the entrance. Gas lamps on either side

of the great doors threw a circle of bright, welcoming light on the area immediately around the steps. But the rest of the courtyard was dark and eerie.

"Wait here," said the vicomte, pushing the door open.

Ben immediately started to follow him. "Sir, you can't go alone —" He stopped because the vicomte's cane was in his chest, pushing him back into his seat.

"I can and I will," the vicomte said firmly. "A large party like ours will only attract attention. Wait here."

"But, sir . . ." Ben tried one last time.

The vicomte gave him an exasperated smile. "Benedict, please, I am a grown man. Allow me *some* adult responsibility." He was smiling to take any sting out of his words, but he still shut the door of the carriage firmly in Ben's face. Ben reluctantly subsided back into his seat as the vicomte turned and walked up the steps.

The friends looked at one another in the gloom of the coach's interior. "Jack," Dominique said tentatively, "tell us what happened after they caught you again?"

Jack shrugged. "There ain't much to tell. They put me back in the cell, only this time they left a guard. I dunno how long I was there—felt like a few hours. Then four vampires came back and made me walk for miles underground. Once it got dark, we came outside and got a coach that took us to the cemetery. Then they blindfolded me and Camazotz joined us."

"Did you see him?" Emily asked.

He shook his head. "No. I heard flapping, you know,

like wings. Then I heard him talk. I guess he—" Jack jumped suddenly and stopped talking. He had seen something out of the corner of his eye—something black, fluttering outside the carriage.

"What is it?" Ben said.

Jack shook his head doubtfully. "Probably nothing. I just thought I saw—"

There was a muffled shout from outside and a thud on the roof of the carriage. The coach shook for a moment as the horses seemed to jump in their traces, but then it stood still again.

The friends looked at one another in alarm.

"What was—" Ben started.

But he was interrupted by a startled cry from Dominique. "Look!"

Lit garishly by the gaslights, red blood was trickling down the outside of the carriage window.

Chapter Twenty-One

They all jumped and instinctively moved away from the blood. But Jack and Ben leaned forward again, craning their necks to try to see up and out of the window.

"Vampires!" Jack whispered. "We got to warn the vicomte."

They strained their ears. Apart from the one shout, there had been no further sound.

"I could go and —" Emily began.

"No," said Ben and Jack together. Emily rolled her eyes.

"I'll go," Jack muttered. "Dominique . . ."

But Dominique was already pressing the talisman of Chac into his hands. "Be safe, Jack," she whispered.

"I will —" Jack started, but Ben suddenly tugged the talisman from his hand. "Hey!"

"You're hurt," Ben said. "I'll do it." And before Jack could protest, he had wrapped the chain of the pendant firmly around his hand and flung the door open.

"Not on your own, you won't," Jack said, and started to follow him. He was aware of the girls getting up behind him. "No, you two stay here."

The girls looked at each other.

"You know we won't stay put," Emily pointed out.

Jack grunted. "All right, come on, then."

Ben stood on the cobbles outside, talisman raised, staring up at the roof of the coach. The horses stood in their traces, and though their sides heaved and their eyes rolled with terror, something stopped them from bolting. It was not the driver. He had fallen back from his seat and now lay across the carriage roof. Two bats crouched over his body. Their faces were at his neck, their leathery wings spread for balance, and their bodies pulsed obscenely as they gorged on the man's blood.

"Get off him, you brutes!" Ben shouted, and swung the talisman at the bats. They veered away sharply, screeching angrily as they swooped up and away into the night.

It seemed the vampires had held the horses in some kind of thrall—Jack remembered the way the coach had jolted, then stopped again—for as soon as the bats had gone, the horses screamed and bolted, taking the coach with them.

"No!" Jack shouted. He ran a few steps after the coach before realizing he would never catch it. The horses were tearing down the Place du Carrousel, back in the direction of the Tuileries. He turned back to the others. "Now what?" he said.

"We have to warn Uncle Henri," Dominique said, looking worried.

"I agree." Ben handed the talisman back. "This is yours, Dominique. Now let's find the vicomte."

It was lucky they had Dominique with them, Jack thought (and *that* was a thought he would not have had twenty-four hours previously). They had only ventured a little way into the dark, deserted galleries before he was hopelessly lost. An occasional lamp lit the junctions of passages and hallways, but the rest was a shadowy maze of crisscrossing corridors and echoing galleries. At any other time he would just have filled his lungs and yelled, "Vicomte!" But now was not a good time for that approach.

Fortunately Dominique could take them straight through the maze and up the stairs to the South American gallery. The square, stone eyes of the Mayan and Aztec carvings stared blankly at them from the shadows. Oil lamps burned on the walls, but their flickering light provided only small pools of light in the vast darkness of the gallery.

"Uncle Henri!" Dominique called. Jack winced at the noise. "Where are you?"

A pause. Then: "In here, my sweet." The vicomte's voice came from the archway that led to his office. "Wait there."

Jack just had time to be surprised that he could hear *two* sets of footsteps approaching, and then the vicomte appeared in the archway. He had taken his coat off and now held it slung over one arm. Jack noticed that cracked, yellow parchments were poking out of one pocket.

But there was someone else with the vicomte—another man, smartly dressed in tails. Jack frowned, because he looked familiar somehow . . . and then his eyes widened as he realized why. "That's the one who hurt me!" he shouted, pointing. He remembered the man from the sewers, and could still feel the place where the man's finger had turned into a claw and driven into his shoulder.

Emily gasped. "Sir, he's the one who brought Camazotz's message to us in the alley!" she exclaimed.

But the vampire and the vicomte were both smiling now. The vampire's grin grew impossibly wide for a human face, and the vicomte's eyes blazed with red fire. "*Bring them to their new master!*" he ordered. His voice was the voice of Camazotz.

Chapter Twenty-Two

"*No!*" Jack screamed in fury. He could hardly believe it: Like Sir Donald Finlay before him, the Vicomte de Montargis was dead, his body now possessed by the vampire god, Camazotz.

And they had traveled in the coach with him!

The vampire was now advancing on them slowly. He opened his arms wide, and his hands began to change into claws. "The master bids you to attend him," he said mockingly in careful English.

Dominique screamed and flung the talisman at him. He twisted to one side and it flew safely past.

Jack and Ben both looked at it. Jack was busy working out exactly how far away it was. No doubt Ben was doing the same. Could they get to it before the creature got to them?

The creature followed their gazes. "Yes, it is a problem, is it not?" he hissed.

"Uncle Henri!" Dominique wailed. Either she hadn't realized the terrible truth, or her mind just would not accept it. "Uncle Henri, you must come away with us now."

She moved toward him, but Emily caught her and held her back. Dominique beat at her with her fists. "Let me go! Let me go now!"

Camazotz's laughter filled the room. "*Yes, let her go. Let her come to her uncle.*" The demon god stood there in the form of the vicomte, arms folded, watching Dominique with amusement.

"Dominique," Emily gasped, struggling to keep hold of the French girl. "That isn't your uncle anymore."

And that was when Jack made his move. He didn't do what the vampire would expect. He didn't run for the talisman. Instead he lunged at the nearest wall and jumped. His fingers reached for the handle of one of the oil lamps, and as he came back down to the ground, he hurled it to the floor in front of the vampire. The glass shattered and burning oil poured out onto the floor. The vampire jumped back, but some of the oil spattered his legs. He swatted at himself to put out the flames.

"Now, Ben!" Jack shouted. But Ben was already moving. With the vampire out of the way, he had flung himself at the talisman and scooped it up. The vampire spun around to face him and Ben advanced on the creature, talisman held out. The vampire howled in frustrated anger. He was caught between the burning oil on one side and the talisman on the other. With an angry shriek, he transformed into a bat and flew off into the dark of the gallery's arched ceiling.

"*Incompetent fool!*" the vicomte bellowed. He flung his

coat down and raised his hands. A mighty blast of cold air rushed through the gallery, instantly extinguishing the blazing oil.

Ben looked around frantically for the vampire bat.

"It's behind you, Ben!" Jack shouted.

Ben turned just in time to see the creature diving toward him. Its vicious white fangs filled his vision. He recoiled and instinctively swung the talisman up at the bat.

The small stone artifact struck the vampire full in the face. White light blazed as the power of the Mayan lightning god, Chac, surged into its enemy. A clap of thunder reverberated around the gallery and the vampire exploded in a cloud of flame and ashes.

Ben immediately wheeled around and flung the talisman at the vicomte with all his strength.

The demon god caught it, snatching it out of the air. He held it up so that it dangled on its chain. "*Very pretty*," he said in a mocking imitation of Jack's voice. "*But it doesn't go with my eyes.*" And with that, he dropped it into his other hand and closed his fingers around it. The stone tablet crumbled, and a small shower of grit fell to the ground.

The vicomte looked up again and his eyes blazed with red fire. "*Too much light,*" he said, looking at the lamps that lined the walls of the gallery. "*I walk by darkness. So shall it be.*" He gestured and, one by one, the lamps down the gallery winked out as the vicomte walked toward the friends.

Dominique stared at the approaching figure with brimming eyes. "He is not . . . ?" she whispered.

Emily put an arm around her. "He is not your uncle, Dominique. I'm sorry."

Dominique began to sob.

Camazotz looked at his enemies. "*The final piece of my amulet will give me power beyond imagining. I will find it. But first, I shall deal with you once and for all,*" he said.

Defenseless, the friends drew closer together as the vicomte advanced on them. Moonlight threw his shadow onto the wall behind him. But as the friends watched, it began to change, swelling and distorting, until something huge and monstrous was looming out of the darkness. Eyes of fire glared down at them.

"Run!" Ben shouted, breaking the spell that held them. As one, they turned and fled toward the exit. Another mighty blast of icy wind swept past them, and the doors ahead slammed shut with a crash.

The inhuman shape of Camazotz bore down on them out of the darkness. "*Your beating hearts shall serve in a ritual that will consolidate my power forever,*" he told them. "*How fitting that the hearts of my enemies should thus prove to make me stronger.*"

"Come this way!" Dominique tugged at Jack's hand and pulled him into a chamber on the right. Ben and Emily followed, while Camazotz's laughter echoed after them. "*Run as fast as you can! My servants hold this building! THERE IS NO ESCAPE!*"

Chapter Twenty-Three

Jack crouched in the corner of a dark room full of ancient pottery. He knew the others were also hiding around the room, but he couldn't see them. Two vampires walked past his hiding place. He pressed himself against the wall and held his breath.

"There are four human children," said a man's voice. Jack noted that the vampire spoke and sounded English, and reflected miserably that Camazotz had clearly brought some of his English converts with him to Paris. "They are to be brought to the master alive. Whoever finds them may feast on them, but they must not be killed."

The other vampire, a woman, hissed eagerly, "Young blood—the best. Do you think they will run?"

The first chuckled horribly. "They will certainly run."

"I love it when they run," the woman said as they walked away. "Do you not relish the smell of their fear?"

"Oh, yes. The quickness of their breath. The pounding of their hearts. All that warm, sweet blood . . ."

Jack kept completely still until they had gone. Then he

slowly emerged from his corner. A sudden movement made him jump, but it was just Dominique coming out from the shadows behind a tall grandfather clock. They looked at each other but said nothing. Dominique's eyes were still red from weeping, but her expression was determined. She hurried across to a chest by the wall and lifted the lid to let Ben and Emily out.

The friends had been hurrying along a landing that overlooked a wide hallway. Fortunately they had seen the shadows of the vampires approaching before the vampires had seen them. That stroke of luck had given them a few precious moments in which to hide.

"Come on," Dominique said.

"No, wait," Jack replied. He faced them all, a determined expression on his face. "You heard that vampire woman talking. She said they can *smell* fear! So we have to try not to be afraid." He took a couple of deep breaths.

The others just looked at him.

"Like me," he urged. "Come on, breathe like me—deep and slow."

Gradually they began to do as he said, matching their breathing to his.

"Just breathe slow and natural," he said. "And get your heartbeat down. It's only Camazotz, ain't it? We *know* we can fight him. It's just a case of finding the right way. Now, concentrate—*we ain't going to be afraid!*" He paused, listening intently. "But we *is* going to run down these stairs, right now," he said. And they did.

There were no vampires on the landing below. The broad stone staircase swept downward into the gloom, and the friends hurried on, anxious to escape the Louvre. Halfway down they came to a small landing. There was a window here, and moonlight poured onto the stone floor. They were just crossing the landing when Jack caught sight of a rash of black shadows out of the corner of his eye. Bats were circling outside. He slowed to a halt.

"Jack!" Ben said urgently. But then he saw what Jack had seen.

Jack pressed his face to the glass and felt it vibrating with the chilling calls of the vampire bats. He craned his neck to look from left to right, up and down. Clouds of black shapes, darker than the night sky, swarmed around the museum. "They're everywhere," he said. "They're coming from *everywhere*."

"Coming to pay homage to their master, now that he has a new body," Ben said grimly.

"We set foot outside this place and they'll have us," Jack muttered.

Something thumped into the window and he jumped back with a yelp. A bat was hovering on the other side of the glass and its tiny red eyes glared at him.

"But they're in here, too," Emily said.

"So we ain't going anywhere," Jack said bluntly. "We 'ave to 'ide."

A slow grin spread across Ben's face, and suddenly he ran back up to the floor above. "Come on!"

The others looked at one another in bewilderment, then followed.

Having checked that there were no vampires present, Ben was running his hands thoughtfully over the wooden panels that lined the landing. "Does this paneling remind you of something?" he asked.

Jack looked at him blankly. "Walls?" he suggested.

"Exactly," Ben agreed, to Jack's evident confusion.

But Emily had caught on. "The secret chamber!" she exclaimed. "Yes! It was somewhere on this floor, I think. But I have no idea where."

Dominique smiled. "I do," she said, setting off along a corridor. "Follow me."

They came to another long gallery with no hiding places at all. Vampire shadows loomed at one end, so they immediately darted into the first room they came to. It was full of medieval weaponry. Rows of pikes and halberds stood along one wall, and the display cases were full of swords and daggers.

They paused for a moment, trying to control their breathing as Jack had shown them. "Thank you, Jack," Ben murmured. "I think this is working."

"So far," Jack muttered.

Ben grinned. "I'm just glad we brought you those clean clothes, or they'd smell you a mile off, fear or no —"

"Mine!" hissed a voice.

The four friends spun around. A man stood in the doorway. His face was almost completely changed into its vampire form. His eyes glowed red and his fangs gleamed in the moonlight. "Mine will be the reward when I present you to the master!"

The vampire paused, perhaps deciding how best to attack. Ben and Jack stood to one side of the room, Dominique and Emily to the other. He must have decided that the girls were an easier target, because he lunged at them. They screamed and dodged to the other side of a table.

Ben picked up a chair and ran at the vampire, who turned just in time to catch the chair as it was about to hit him and shoved it back. Ben and the chair flew across the room and Ben thudded into the wall. There was a pike mounted on it, just above his head: a heavy pole, with a sharp spear point at one end. Ben grabbed hold of it and pulled it down, staggering under its weight.

The vampire was still advancing on the girls.

"Jack! Help me!" Ben yelled. Jack was already on his way. The boys held the pike between them and ran at the vampire. He looked around in surprise but didn't have time to dodge before the point pierced his chest and drove him back against the wall. The spearhead ran right through the vampire's body and embedded itself in the oak paneling.

The boys slowly stepped away from it. The vampire looked down at the spear that pinned him. Then he wrapped his hands around the shaft and tugged. The pike remained stuck in the wall.

"Foolish," the vampire said, and to the friends' horror, he began to move. He walked forward, letting the spear slide through his torso. "It takes more than that to kill a vam—"

With a cry, Dominique swung an ax at the vampire. The blade sliced cleanly through his neck and his head dropped to the floor with a thud. The body went limp, dangling from the shaft of the spear.

"But chopping your head off does the trick, eh?" Jack said conversationally. The words dried in his mouth, however, for as he spoke, the headless vampire's legs straightened and he picked himself up. He began to move forward again, relentlessly, until his body came clear of the shaft.

Dominique had forgotten she was holding an ax. She stood transfixed by the sight of a headless corpse reaching out for her. Worse, Jack could see her drawing breath for a mighty scream that would surely bring the entire army of vampires down upon them.

But before she could make a noise, the vampire lunged toward her. Emily pulled Dominique out of the way just in time. The vampire staggered slightly but righted himself quickly and leapt between the girls and the door. He stood, crouched, arms and talons outstretched. He seemed to be deciding which one to go for next.

"But how does it know where they are?" Ben gasped. "How can it see?"

"Dunno," Jack replied. "Its eyes are . . ." He glanced down at where the head had fallen and recoiled in horror. The eyes blazed up at him with hatred, and they were moving. Sickeningly, unbelievably, the head was still alive, and it was still controlling the body.

Jack didn't hesitate. He picked the head up by the hair and looked around desperately for somewhere to put it.

"In here!" Ben shouted, pulling a wooden chest open. Jack pitched the head in and Ben slammed the lid shut on top of it. He grabbed a sword off the wall and slid its blade through the hasp of the lock, pinning the lid down.

Now blind, the headless vampire staggered vaguely in the direction of the girls, arms flailing. The friends moved cautiously around the edges of the room to the exit, then fled.

Dominique led them flawlessly, but it was hard to stay hidden as they ran from room to room. Several times they had to dart back into a corridor or hide behind a display as vampires stalked the galleries. Every time the friends reached a junction, they had to peer cautiously around the corners to ensure their way was clear. It slowed them down considerably, but it was essential. The vampires seemed to be quartering the museum very systematically, searching every room until they found their quarry.

Dominique had to get them to the secret chamber quickly. "In here," she said. Jack looked around. It was just as he remembered it—a small room, lined with paintings in gold frames.

Ben was already by the fireplace, running his hands over the carved mantel. "Where was it? Where was it?" he muttered.

"Ben, *hurry*!" Emily whispered. They could all hear footsteps approaching.

"The crown, there, the monogram," Dominique hissed. The carving on the dark wood was difficult to make out in the gloom. Ben frantically ran his fingers over the surface.

Suddenly there was a click and a square black hole appeared in one wall. Ben gestured at his friends. "Get in! Quick!"

Emily and Dominique were inside in a flash.

Jack hung back. "If they find us in this chamber, we're trapped," he pointed out.

Ben nodded. "But remember," he said, "the vicomte told us he hadn't been on the tour we took. That means Camazotz probably won't know the secret chamber exists!"

"Something old clever clogs don't know!" Jack said, brightening. "Good." He slipped inside with Emily and Dominique. Ben clambered in, too, and pulled the door shut. It was pitch-black in the secret chamber. The friends couldn't see a thing, but after a few moments they heard footsteps enter the room.

"Are they there?" asked a muffled voice on the other side of the panel, and Jack recognized the voice of the English vampire he had overheard earlier.

"No," his female companion replied.

The second speaker was standing so close to the secret door that Ben nearly jumped out of his skin. A stray mote of dust went up his nose, and with horror he felt a desperate urge to sneeze growing inside him. He pinched his nose, willing the sneeze away.

"There is nowhere in here to hide," the woman continued, "unless . . . wait, what is this?"

Jack held his breath, and he was sure the others did, too. The secret chamber was silent as a grave.

"What are you doing?" asked the male vampire.

"I thought they might be up the chimney," the woman responded, sounding disappointed. "But they cannot be. It is too narrow."

"Then we must keep looking," the man said, sounding worried. "We do not want to face the master's wrath. . . ."

The hours passed unbearably slowly for the friends in their cramped hiding place. Ben guessed it must have been shortly after one o'clock in the morning when they had first entered the secret chamber. He knew they could not leave until sunrise. Every hour he heard the distant sound of a clock chiming. Many times during the night he heard footsteps and voices outside. The vampires were growing more and more angry and frustrated. Ben could imagine why—the wrath of Camazotz was a terrible thing indeed.

Shortly before seven o'clock the awful voice of Camazotz thundered through the museum. "*You have not found them? You FOOLS!*"

The floorboards shook with the force of Camazotz's fury.

"*You sniveling . . .*"

Ben heard the hideous scream of a dying vampire as Camazotz turned his rage on his own servants.

"*. . . pathetic . . .*" More shrieks and wails from vampires echoed around the galleries.

"*. . . incompetent . . .*"

Dust trickled down from the ceiling and Ben felt overwhelmingly thankful that Camazotz's servants hadn't discovered the hidden chamber.

"*FOOLS!*"

The thunder died away and the paneling stopped vibrating. Ben pressed his ear to the wood to listen and jumped as Camazotz spoke again.

"*Do you hear me, boy? You and your friends? You think you have outwitted me. But the vicomte could not stand against me and I will destroy you, too. Do you hear me? I WILL DESTROY YOU!*"

And then there was silence.

"I can't hear anything," Ben whispered. "Does anyone remember what time the sun comes up?" No one did. Ben sighed into the darkness. "Well, we're not leaving this hiding place until we're absolutely sure it's daylight outside. So settle down and make yourselves comfortable."

It seemed to Ben only minutes later that he was being shaken awake by Jack. He had managed to curl up and sleep, resting his head on his rolled-up coat. He opened his eyes to absolute darkness. He could see nothing, but he could hear voices on the other side of the wood. He listened intently, wondering if it was still dark outside, wondering if the vampires were still hunting them. The voices came closer.

And then Ben grinned in the darkness, and he heard his friends sigh with relief. Because they all recognized the voice they could hear.

"Come on," Ben said. "I think we're about to be let out."

"You see this carving here?" said a voice in French on the other side of the secret door. "You see the monogram of Louis XIII? Well, you press it and . . ."

There was a *click* and the wooden door panel swung open. Daylight flooded into the secret chamber and the friends blinked in the sudden glare. Gaston, the guide, stood with his back to the cubbyhole as he spoke to a party of elderly ladies and gentlemen. Ben saw the guests lean down to peer into the chamber. They drew back in surprise when they saw Ben, Emily, Jack, and Dominique.

"It is said that the Cardinal Richelieu . . ." Gaston was saying.

"Good morning, Gaston," Dominique said brightly as she climbed out through the doorway, followed by the other three. Gaston nearly jumped halfway across the room in shock.

"We, um, got a bit lost?" Emily said, by way of explanation.

"But it was an excellent tour," Ben added, following his sister.

"Very educational," Jack agreed, bringing up the rear.

Chapter Twenty-Four

They drew a few curious stares from onlookers as they made their way through the grand corridors of the Louvre, as they were somewhat grimy and rumpled from their time in the secret chamber. Their steps took them past the South American gallery. It was strange to see it still in some disrepair.

"They have not finished clearing it up yet," Dominique said in surprise.

"It's only been a day," Ben said glumly, and it was a shock to all of them. Only a day! Only twenty-four hours since they had found Professor Adensnap murdered! It felt like a month.

"We've failed, haven't we?" Jack said gloomily. "We're no closer to defeating Camazotz."

Ben was quiet for a moment. When he spoke, there was a note of icy resolve in his voice that none of them had ever heard before. "No," he said. "We haven't failed yet. We know where Camazotz will go once he's read the parchments. He'll go to find the fourth piece of the amulet."

"So he'll go to Mexico," Jack said. Then he realized

what Ben had in mind. "You want to go to Mexico?" he asked incredulously.

Ben shrugged. "We want to find the fourth piece before Camazotz can get ahold of it, don't we? As far as we know, it's still in the Yucatán."

"Mexico . . ." Jack breathed in wonder. That was the kind of place he had always dreamed of visiting. A place of exotic jungles and ancient mysteries . . . But he could see a problem. "Stop me if I'm wrong," he said, "'cos you been there and I haven't, and all, but . . . ain't Mexico a big kind of place? Where we going to start looking?"

"I've no idea," said Ben frankly. "If we still had the parchments, perhaps we could find out, but now *he* has them."

Emily cleared her throat significantly. They all turned to her and were surprised to see a big smile on her face. "Do you mean *these* parchments?" she asked.

Simultaneously Jack, Ben, and Dominique shifted their gaze to Emily's right hand, in which she held some old, yellowing pages.

Ben stared at them doubtfully for a moment, uncertain whether he could believe his eyes. "That's . . . those can't be them!" he exclaimed. "We . . . we saw them in the vicomte's pocket."

"Yes, they *were* in his pocket," Emily agreed. "But while you boys were having fun fighting the vampire . . ."

"Fun, eh?" Jack muttered. "Can't say it were the most fun I ever —"

". . . I took them out and replaced them with another old parchment from my bag."

"So . . . so what does Camazotz have?" Ben asked.

"Some very dry and boring stuff about Mayan agriculture," Emily said, "which I expect he already knows. I brought the parchment to Paris to show it to the vicomte."

"Well, in that case," Jack said, laughing, "let's go to Mexico!" Then he frowned. "But how do we *get* to Mexico? It ain't going to be cheap."

There was a small cough, and Emily, Ben, and Jack suddenly remembered Dominique. They turned to face her. She was still with them, looking rather forlorn.

"Oh, Dominique, I'm sorry," Emily said. "We were being thoughtless."

"You could . . ." Jack was surprised to hear the words coming out of his own mouth. "You could come with us, too, eh?"

Dominique shook her head. "I cannot. My father died long ago. Now that Uncle Henri is gone, I am all my mother has left. I must return to her. But come with me—there is something I must show you."

They glanced at one another, then followed Dominique through the arch that led to the vicomte's office. Dominique crossed to the desk and opened a drawer. "It is still here," she said. "I did not think Camazotz would be interested in this kind of thing." She pulled out a small bag that clinked as it moved. She had to hold it with both hands as she tipped it over on the desktop. A mass of gold coins spilled out.

"I remembered the gendarme mentioning these," Dominique explained. She counted the coins quickly. There were one hundred of them, each made of solid gold. "Four thousand francs," she said. "I think that will get you to Mexico."

"Dominique, are you sure?" Ben asked. "They were your uncle's."

"What else can he do with them?" Dominique said simply. "Use them to stop . . ." Her voice shook slightly. "Use them to stop his murderer."

"Thank you, Dominique," Emily said softly. "The money will be a great help."

"Absolutely," Jack agreed. "Thanks, Dominique." Dominique's face lit up at Jack's words and the warmth in his voice.

"So," Ben said decisively. "Now that we have the money, we have to plan exactly how we're going to avoid Camazotz and get to Mexico!"

Chapter Twenty-Five

Emily laid down her pen and stretched. She sat back in her chair and moved her shoulders to ease the knots out of her back. The others waited with bated breath for her to speak.

They were in the hotel suite Professor Adensnap had originally booked for them. It was very comfortable, with a high ceiling and a grand chandelier. The walls were covered with gold silk and the main window looked out onto the busy Rue de Rivoli and the majestic Louvre itself.

"The fourth piece was hidden in another temple," Emily said. She smiled. "Where else?"

"And the vicomte said no other artifacts like the bat or the eye had been found," Ben pointed out.

"Exactly," agreed Emily. "Which is why I think it's probably still there!"

"Can you find it?" Dominique asked.

"The exact location may be given somewhere in these parchments," Emily said. "But I don't know. And it will take a long time for me to translate everything. Even if I can work out in which temple the crescent moon was hidden, from what Ben's told me about how overgrown the jungle is, we could walk right past the temple without even noticing."

"We'll worry about that when we get there," Ben said firmly. "But first . . . Jack, look."

He and Jack moved over to the window and stood on either side of it so they couldn't be seen. Then they craned their necks to peer down at the street below. Curious, Emily and Dominique peered out, too, careful to keep out of sight, as the boys were doing.

A figure lounged against the wall on the other side of the Rue de Rivoli. It was a small boy in a coat that was much too big for him.

"Is that him?" Ben said.

"That's the one." Jack scowled at the boy. "He led me into the vampires' trap, he did."

"Camazotz can't move about in daylight, which is why not all his servants are vampires," Ben said. "That little brat can lead him straight to us, wherever we go. And he'll know we have the real documents by now."

"It should not be hard to trick him," Dominique said. "Now that we know he is there."

Jack shook his head. "He's just the one we can see," he said, turning away from the window. "Camazotz ain't stupid. He puts someone like that right in front of us, so we think we've sussed his game. Then the others will sneak up behind us when we're not looking. It's an old trick."

"And how many old tricks do you know, Jack?" Ben asked with a laugh.

Jack grinned. "More than him, I'm betting."

Jack, Dominique, and Emily left the hotel and walked slowly east along the Rue de Rivoli, past the Louvre.

"I hope your brother will recover soon," Dominique said loudly.

"Yes," said Emily. "His health has always been fragile. All this excitement has been bad for him. But he will need his strength for our journey to Spain."

"To *Spain*, Emily?" Dominique asked.

"Yes, Dominique. To *Spain*," Emily reiterated. "That is where we need to go."

Jack groaned to himself. Both girls had had an expensive education, but obviously it hadn't included acting lessons. Nonetheless, it was important that the spies heard them talking about Spain. To get to the Americas, the friends would need to head north to a French port; Ben reckoned it would be Le Havre. Therefore they wanted to make Camazotz think that they were going in precisely the opposite direction. Without the parchments, Camazotz still needed their knowledge. Wherever they went, he would follow.

"We will need to go to the Gare d'Austerlitz if you are

to take the train to Spain," said Dominique. "We traveled to Spain last summer, my cousin and I, and he had terrible stomach pains when he ate a shellfish. We had gone to see the Alhambra palace, and it was very bad—I mean the shellfish, not the palace. The palace had never been near the sea, but neither had the shellfish, I think. It was built by the Moors in the thirteenth century, I mean the palace, of course, because the Moors would never build a shellfish, that would be silly. . . ."

Jack sighed loudly to bring her attention back.

"Oh . . . yes, and so you must buy tickets at the Gare d'Austerlitz," Dominique finished, coming back to the script they had prepared earlier.

"Yes. We will. And you must buy a ticket to Toulon," Emily replied.

"While you go to Spain," Dominique added, in case it wasn't clear.

"Yes."

Jack decided they had walked far enough from the hotel. He put his foot up on a post and casually untied his shoelaces. Then he just as casually tied them up again. At the same time he glanced under his arm, back the way they had come. It gave him an upside-down view of the crowds in the Rue de Rivoli—which was enough for him to spot the small figure trailing them, and another besides.

"What do you see?" Emily asked quietly.

"The lad's taken the bait," Jack said as he straightened

up. "'E's following us. So's a bloke in a long coat and a 'at who thinks we ain't seen 'im."

"Where?" Emily immediately inquired, glancing back.

"I *said*, 'e *thinks* we *ain't seen 'im*," Jack hissed, and Emily quickly looked away.

"Sorry, Jack," she said.

"You are very clever to know these things, Jack," Dominique put in admiringly.

Jack grinned reluctantly. "I ain't always been a gent," he told her. "C'mon. We can get a cab now we know they're onto us."

They hailed a carriage and climbed in. Jack was the last up, and he casually scratched the back of his head. As he did so, he made sure they were being followed.

"*La Gare d'Austerlitz, s'il vous plaît*," Dominique said to the driver.

"For Spain," Jack added under his breath.

Ben, who was peering out of the hotel window, saw Jack scratch his head. It was Jack's signal that the spies had taken the bait and were following him.

"Right," Ben murmured. He patted his pocket to check that the money was still there, swung his coat over his shoulder, and hurried out of the hotel room.

The corridor was lit by gas lamps, which shed a soft glow

on the plush red carpet and the portraits on the walls. Halfway along the passage, a grand staircase led down to the foyer. Ben ignored it and walked on to the far end of the corridor where he passed through a simple white wooden door. As he had guessed, he found himself on the servants' staircase. The decor was much simpler back here in the parts of the hotel that the guests weren't expected to see.

Ben hurried downstairs, his boots clattering on the bare wooden steps. At one point he passed a chambermaid with a pile of clean linen, who looked surprised to see a nicely dressed young man, obviously a guest, on the servants' stairs.

He gave her his most charming smile and put a finger to his lips. "*C'est un jeu!*" he whispered without stopping. *It's a game!*

"Ah!" she said, with a benevolent smile, and she went on her way, chuckling. Ben sucked in his cheeks and hurried on.

The same ploy got him through the staff pantry and the hotel kitchens. He came out in a grimy backstreet that was lined with trash cans and immediately made his way northward, using a string of alleys so that he could avoid the front of the hotel and the Rue de Rivoli.

Finally, he emerged into the Rue de Richelieu, feeling fairly confident that he had done enough to evade any spies who might not have already followed Jack, Emily, and Dominique. He flagged down a cab and asked to go directly to the offices of the shipping company Voyages Trans-atlantiques.

"Tonight?" Ben exclaimed an hour later, half of him delighted and half of him trying to work out if they could possibly get there in time.

The shipping company occupied a large, shadowy hall off the Place de la Madeleine. Bored-looking clerks sat at dusty desks in the echoing space, surrounded by piles of shipping timetables and manifests. The clerk Ben had been speaking to, a middle-aged man with a melancholic air and a twirly mustache, shrugged. "You asked for the ship that would leave soonest, monsieur," he said in French. "And that would be the *Bernadette*, sailing tonight at nine o'clock from Le Havre to New Orleans in the United States. The next scheduled sailing will be a month from now. Therefore, if you want to travel quickly, you must travel tonight."

The man tapped the map laid out between them. Ben could see that the Yucatán Peninsula was due south across the Gulf of Mexico from New Orleans. "I regret we do not offer a steam service all the way to Mexico," the clerk said.

Ben stared at the man, hardly daring to believe his ears. "Did you say a *steam* service?" he asked, wondering whether—in the effort of conversing in French—he had misunderstood. He had been expecting to *sail* to Mexico—

a far slower journey. If they could travel by steam before Camazotz could find out and take the same ship, it would give them quite a head start.

"That is correct." The man smiled proudly. "We are a progressive company, monsieur. We have nothing but the best. And once you reach New Orleans, I have no doubt you will find a boat to carry you across the Gulf to the Yucatán." He checked another timetable, running his finger down the columns of small print. Then he looked at his watch. "You will need to take the train to Le Havre from the Gare Saint-Lazare by three o'clock."

Ben glanced at the clock on the wall. It was just coming up to eleven. They had a lot to squeeze into four hours. He was delighted that a ship was leaving so soon. He was concerned that it meant he had to round up Jack and Emily and get them on the train as soon as possible—and somehow manage this without being seen by any of Camazotz's spies.

But steamers didn't have to worry about the vagaries of wind and tide, and if Camazotz missed this one . . . well, he would have to wait a month for the next. Or sail. He would never be able to fly to Mexico in one night, before the sunlight got him.

"We'll take it," Ben said decisively. "Three tickets, please."

The clerk reached for his forms. "Will you be returning?" he asked.

Ben looked at him blankly.

"Do you require return tickets, monsieur?" the clerk said again, speaking slowly in case Ben was struggling with the French. "Are you emigrating to Mexico"— he gave a little cough to show he intended this as a joke —"or do you intend to come back one day?"

Ben realized that the clerk could have no idea of the thoughts he had just sent whirling through Ben's mind. He thought of the huge number of people who had died at the hands of Camazotz and his vampires so far. And he realized that he, or Jack, or Emily, might be added to that list. It might be that none of them would come back from Mexico, for reasons that he could never explain to this man.

So Ben looked him in the eye and said, "*Oui, s'il vous plaît.*" Yes, they would be returning. This time they would defeat Camazotz, once and for all. Ben had to believe that.

Chapter Twenty-Six

Shortly after noon, the door to the hotel room opened and Jack, Emily, and Dominique walked in, chatting happily. They stopped in surprise when they saw Ben in the midst of packing for all of them.

"Where have you *been*?" Ben demanded as he stuffed a pile of shirts into Jack's bag.

"Doing what we was supposed to," Jack replied, a little bemusedly. "We got us booked on a train to Spain."

"And we sent a telegram to Mrs. Mills," put in Emily, "just to say we would be staying away longer than planned."

"And we made sure the spies saw everything," added Dominique. "They think you are going to Spain and I am going to Toulon."

"Good," Ben said, and there was excitement in his voice as he gave them his own news. "Well, I've got us booked on a ship to America. It leaves tonight, and that means *we* have to leave right now!"

They were completely open about the first stage of the journey. Camazotz's spies all had to think they were heading for Spain, and that meant going to the Gare d'Austerlitz in the southeast part of the city. They made as much fuss as they could in checking out of the hotel. Ben insisted on going through the bill twice, even though it was all very straightforward. They didn't want anyone to be in any doubt that they were leaving.

Meanwhile Emily supervised the porters who carried their bags down from the room and piled them up on the pavement. They included Professor Adensnap's cases in the pile, though it broke their hearts. Then Emily insisted that one of the hotel porters signal a cab for them, simply because it would be more noticeable that way.

Finally they were on their way to the station, crammed together in a small cab with the luggage lashed to the roof in a tottering pile.

The Gare d'Austerlitz was a vast engine shed, with long, parallel platforms full of light and noise. The voices of passengers and the hissing of the trains echoed down from the ornate steel-and-glass roof.

The friends made their way to the train for Spain. It was waiting at its platform, steam hissing from the boiler, looking like an impatient metal dragon. Behind it were the smart and comfortable first-class carriages, followed by second class and lastly, third class, open to all weather. The passengers here sat on basic wooden benches. They were well wrapped up against the elements, ready for a twelve-hour journey exposed to the October weather.

At the end of the train was the luggage van. The friends made absolutely sure that anybody watching would see their bags being loaded up.

"That's right, pile 'em in," Jack said, and casually plucked a small, light bag off the top of the pile. He kept it with him as they strolled down the platform to their seats at the front of the train. This was almost the final part of the ruse. They had packed the bare essentials that they would need for the trip to Mexico into this small bag. They were going to the Yucatán, for no one knew how long, with less baggage than they had brought for a week's stay in Paris. Everything was different now. The rest of their bags would go all the way to Spain—probably never to be seen again. But it was a sacrifice that had to be made.

They picked their way through the crowds. Jack turned to speak to the others. As he did so, he casually glanced back down the platform and was very pleased to see the older spy watching them from a distance. He seemed to be the only one.

"We're being followed," he said quietly.

"Good," Ben said. He stopped a porter and showed the man their tickets, asking for their carriage. It was the next one along from where they stood, as Ben already knew, but he wanted to be sure the spy didn't miss seeing them board the train.

The porter politely showed them to the open door of their carriage, and they all climbed in. They found themselves in a narrow corridor that ran along the compartments, ending in a small lobby area. They stood here, preparing themselves for the next stage of their journey and reluctantly saying good-bye to Dominique, who would soon catch her own train to Toulon.

Jack, Ben, and Emily looked at the French girl who had become their friend. She bit her lip and blinked back tears.

"Well . . . good-bye, Dominique," Ben said awkwardly. "Thank you for all your help."

"Good-bye, Ben, Emily . . ." Dominique replied. Then she suddenly flung her arms around Jack. "Good-bye, Jack, my courageous English knight," she said with a brave smile, though her voice shook. She kissed him on both cheeks. "Will you write to me?"

"Soon as I learn how," Jack promised, leaning down to give her a kiss himself, and reflecting that Dominique had changed a lot in the very short time they had known each other.

"Is the spy on board, Jack?" Emily was saying.

"Got on when we did, four carriages down," Jack confirmed.

"So, Dominique, you'll be safe to go and get your *own*

train," Emily finished. "But don't leave the station until you see *this* train go."

"I will not," Dominique said. A whistle from the guard at the end of the train was answered by a whistle from the driver. "Well, perhaps you should get off now?" she added.

Ben nodded and opened the door on the other side of the carriage. There was a five-foot drop straight down to the tracks. He gave Dominique one last wink and jumped down.

Emily was next; Ben reached up to catch her and swing her down. Then Jack dropped the bag down after them and jumped out himself. Emily and Ben were already crawling between the train's wheels. Underneath the train was the one and only place they could guarantee the spy wouldn't see them.

Jack's and Dominique's eyes met for the last time as he looked up at her from the tracks. She gave a last, brave smile. "Good-bye, Jack," she said. He winked and touched his forehead, and she reached out and shut the door.

Jack ducked down and crawled underneath the carriage. He and Ben and Emily looked at one another. None of them said a word. Jack wondered if they were thinking the same as he—*What on earth am I doing under here?*

"Good-bye, Ben! Good-bye, Emily!"

They could just hear Dominique's voice. She was maintaining the show until the last minute. They could see her feet on the platform. She had disembarked and was now waving enthusiastically at the nonexistent passengers who had supposedly remained on board. "I will miss you!"

There were more whistles, a final shriek from the engine, and the train began to move. Jack pressed himself into the gravel between the rails as hundreds of tons of steel began to pass by above him. The smell of oil and grease and hot metal stuck in his throat and filled his nose. The wheels sighed and sang along the metal tracks, which thrummed like the strings of a mighty guitar. And the whole chain of coaches and carriages creaked and groaned overhead. It was terrifying. Jack knew that there were several feet of clearance between himself and the train. As long as he kept low, it would pass by harmlessly. But it felt as if the world were collapsing on top of him slowly, bit by bit. The noise and the dust and the heat overwhelmed him until he thought it would never end.

But then it was gone. The noise was behind him and receding, and sunlight blazed down. Jack slowly opened his eyes. He had no memory of having shut them.

Ben and Emily looked at him slowly and smiled. Then all three of them got to their feet.

A shocked porter in the railway company uniform was glaring down at them, and a small crowd was gathering. The three friends looked quite a sight. Not only were they on the tracks, but their clothes were grimy with dust and oil.

Ben coped with the attention by simply ignoring it.

"Time to head for Saint-Lazare," he said firmly as he brushed himself down. "Just act normally."

And so they climbed back up onto the platform. Jack and Ben went first, throwing the bag ahead of them and then reaching down to haul Emily up, too. There was no sign of Dominique. She had obviously followed her instructions and walked away once the train had left, as if her three English friends were really on it.

"Right, we'll just walk to the exit, looking as calm and dignified as possible," Emily muttered.

"Calm and dignified," Jack said with a grin. "You got it."

Ben reached into his pocket and pulled out his watch. "It's twenty past two. We have forty minutes to catch our real train," he said. "Run!"

They left "calm and dignified" on the station platform and fled for the exit.

Chapter Twenty-Seven

Ben, Jack, and Emily were in a carriage rattling through the streets of Paris. They had thirty minutes to get across the city, buy tickets, and get on board the train. Ben had given the driver double the fare to get them there as fast as possible, and the driver was taking his work seriously. The coach hurtled around a tight bend, and the three friends were thrown across the cab.

"Good-bye, Paris, eh?" Jack said with a smile. Ben and Emily smiled back as the carriage pulled up outside the Gare Saint-Lazare with only minutes to spare. Jack and Emily ran on ahead to the train while Ben bought the tickets. Luckily, the line was short and Ben was soon pushing his way through the crowds and running for the train.

He found Jack and Emily arguing with a guard, who wanted to close the carriage door and let the train move off. They were adamantly holding the door open.

"Ben! Thank goodness!" Emily said as her brother arrived. The guard drew breath to harangue Ben for holding everyone up.

"Do you want the train to go or don't you?" Ben

demanded as he jumped on board. The guard must have decided that letting the train go was more important than moaning at Ben. Muttering under his breath, he waved a green flag, and the train shuddered into motion.

At long last, the friends felt they could relax. They sank back into the padded horsehair seats with sighs of relief.

"We gave Camazotz's spy the slip all right, didn't we?" Jack said with a proud smile. He glanced out the window as the platform slipped by and suddenly sat bolt upright. "I don't believe it!" he groaned.

The first thing he had noticed was the coat. It was too big for its wearer and the hem trailed on the ground. Inside it was the small boy who had led Jack into the sewers and who had been spying on the friends in the hotel. He was lounging against an iron pillar, and his eyes met Jack's as the train sped past. He smiled cheekily and gave a mock salute, then turned and sauntered away down the platform.

The train rumbled slowly along the valley of the river Seine toward Le Havre, in the dim light of the dying afternoon. The river wound and twisted its way around them as they went. Sometimes it ran alongside the track, sometimes it disappeared in the ever-deepening gloom. There was still over an hour to go until sunset, but the clouds blocked the sun and the friends felt as though evening was upon them.

"We don't know that the lad's still working for

Camazotz," Jack pointed out hopefully. "He could've been working alone."

"Then what was he doing at the station?" Ben demanded.

"Plenty of rich people with full pockets what don't button down," Jack said reasonably. "A boy's got to eat."

"Ben, you had to buy tickets for the ship," Emily put in. "Maybe Camazotz will, too. That will slow him down. And how often do the trains run to Le Havre?"

"More often than steamships run to America," Ben growled.

"Well, what can we do about it while we're on this train?" Emily asked.

"Nothing!" Ben replied in a whisper, and Jack knew this meant he was overwrought.

"Exactly," Emily said sensibly. "So let's enjoy the ride and hope for the best, shall we?"

The train pulled into Le Havre at seven o'clock that evening, well after sunset. It settled itself in front of the buffers and steam rushed out of its boiler. It gave off the satisfied air of a job well done.

Ben was on the platform even before the train had stopped moving. "Come on, come on!" he urged. Jack and Emily had stopped reminding him that the ship didn't sail until nine o'clock. They glanced at each other and rolled their eyes, but they stepped down onto the platform and followed Ben without comment.

Customs here was just like Customs in Calais. Whether you were sailing across the English Channel or the Atlantic Ocean, the rules were much the same. The friends shuffled slowly forward in the line of passengers until they were able to put their one bag up onto the table for inspection.

The customs officer looked at the bag, then at the three children it belonged to. "This is all your luggage?" he asked in surprise.

"Everything else is on board," Emily said quickly. "Our uncle took it with him."

"*Bon. D'accord,*" was all the man said. He marked the bag with his stick of chalk, and they were through.

The *Bernadette* was twice the size of the Dover ferry. It had six masts and four funnels. When the wind blew in the right direction, the crew would hoist the sails and the ship would travel under sail alone, to save fuel. Its sides were lined with portholes and each one blazed with a cheerful light.

It was truly dark now and a cold wind blew in off the sea. Jack, in particular, felt the cold, since he no longer had a coat. He pulled his jacket around him for warmth and let the hustle and bustle of the ship distract him. The brightly lit vessel was like a beacon of hope and warmth ahead of him.

The friends didn't go straight up onto the deck. A gangplank led in through an open hatch in the side of the ship. Inside, the ship's crew, in white uniforms, checked their tickets and showed them the way to their shared cabin. It was much more formal than the Channel crossing.

The cabin had a small basin and four bunks, two on either side, one above the other. It was warm and snug and Jack relished being out of the wind. There was a porthole covered by a white lace curtain. It was on the port side of the ship, away from the dock and facing out to sea. Jack stooped to peer through it. "This is all right, isn't it?" he said happily.

"Not yet," Ben replied grimly, somewhat dampening Jack's high spirits. "I'm going up on deck." He turned and left the cabin.

Emily glanced at Jack. "I should go with him," she said with a sigh, and followed.

Jack took a final, longing look at the cozy cabin, then buttoned up his jacket and went after his friends.

Jack and Emily found Ben leaning against the rail, just aft of the paddle housing, staring out at Le Havre.

"Any sign of Camazotz or his vampires?" Emily asked in hushed tones.

Ben shook his head and pulled his watch from his pocket. "Eight o'clock," he said. "He's still got an hour."

They settled down to wait. By half past eight there was still no sign of Camazotz. Ben was pacing the deck anxiously, but he never went far and he kept his eyes on the shore. Every man or woman who headed toward the ship was carefully studied, and every cart that rolled along the dock had to be closely scrutinized.

Other passengers were coming up on deck now, laughing and chatting and waving at friends and relatives left behind on the dock. The three friends formed a small island of anxiety amid the general happiness and good cheer.

At five to nine, Ben suddenly ran to the side of the ship and peered out into the darkness. "Oh, no," he whispered. "Oh, no." He wasn't looking at anyone on shore, he was staring up into the air. Emily and Jack followed his gaze, expecting to see a flock of bats descending, but the sky was empty.

"What is it?" Emily asked.

"Can't you feel it?" Ben hissed. "Can't you *feel* it?"

"Feel wh—" Jack began, when the ship suddenly shook and all three clutched at their hats as a sudden blast of wind threatened to snatch them away. A strong, cold breeze had sprung up, blowing across the ocean and striking the port side of the ship. The *Bernadette* was pressed hard against the dockside.

"*That*," Ben whispered, his eyes wild and unfocused. "Camazotz is close. He's almost here. He did it in Mexico and he's doing it again now. He can control the wind. He can make it hold us here until he arrives!"

From Ben's eyes, Jack could tell that his friend wasn't entirely on board the *Bernadette*. Part of him was back on the English ship that had carried him—and Camazotz—from Puerto Morelos to England. *Ben's voice was rising in panic, which was unusual*, Jack thought, *because Ben* never *panicked.*

"Look over here, Ben," Jack said gently. He took Ben's shoulders and guided him, protesting, away from the rail, over to the other side of the *Bernadette*. "They've been tying themselves on for the last ten minutes."

Ben looked down at the two little steam tugs that hovered by the *Bernadette*'s bow. Strong, powerful hawsers ran from their stern decks up to the foredeck of the bigger ship.

Down on the dock, dockhands could be seen unlooping ropes from the bollards that held the ship in place. On board the *Bernadette*, crewmen hauled in the ropes, raised the gangplank, and closed the hatch in the steamer's side. From the ship's horn came a rumbling bellow that made Jack wince and cover his ears.

The tugs slowly headed out to sea. The hawsers straightened, tightened, and the *Bernadette* began to follow. The deck trembled beneath Jack's feet as the big ship slowly peeled itself away from the dock. The wind gusted suddenly, howling around the ship in fury and blowing twice as strongly, but the tugs didn't even seem to notice.

Gradually the *Bernadette*'s own paddles began to turn and a deep thrumming pulsed through the ship as the engines engaged. The *Bernadette* moved through the water awkwardly at first. Every beat of its paddles against the waves threw up gallons of spray and foam and took the steamer a little farther out to sea. The ship was heading into the Baie de la Seine and, after that, the mighty Atlantic.

"We're moving!" Ben cried, his face alight with excitement and relief. "We're moving!" He laughed and hugged first Jack, then Emily. "We're off! Let's go and watch!" And he ran merrily back to the stern of the ship to watch France disappear into the distance.

Emily and Jack smiled at each other.

"Let's keep 'im company," Jack suggested. They started to walk along the deck. Suddenly Jack stopped and grabbed his stomach. A whiff of burned oil and fetid bilge-water had found its way to Jack's nose. He could feel his innards rearranging themselves in a horribly familiar way. "Oh, no!" he protested, but he was already running for the side of the ship.

Chapter Twenty-Eight

An hour later, Jack was still hanging over the stern rail of the *Bernadette*, feeling ill. Above him, the French tricolor waved proudly from the flagstaff as the lights of Le Havre slowly receded. He felt a hand on his shoulder. Ben and Emily had come to join him.

"How long 'ave we got?" Jack moaned.

"Oh, days and days and days," Ben replied cheerfully. Jack groaned and slumped over the rail again. Then he felt something warm around his shoulders and realized that Ben had surrendered his coat.

Emily gave her brother a sharp nudge with her elbow. "Don't tease him," she said, holding out a piece of crystallized ginger. "Here you are, Jack. I bought a good supply of this from the purser."

Jack took it gratefully. "Thanks," he said, putting it in his mouth. Truth to tell, he already felt better. The initial queasiness was passing as he gradually adjusted to the ship's motion. Jack had always been good at adapting to new circumstances, given time.

"Do you think you could bear to go back to the cabin yet?" asked Emily. "It's nice and warm and dry."

Jack managed a weak smile. "Just give me a little while longer," he replied.

The three leaned companionably against the rail together, looking back toward France. Jack regarded the country with decidedly mixed feelings. On the one hand he had lost a dear and irreplaceable friend there, in the shape of Professor Adensnap. On the other hand—much to his surprise—he had made a new one, in the shape of Dominique.

He glanced across at Ben and Emily and guessed that they probably felt much the same. Jack smiled. *In spite of the uneasy feeling in his stomach*, he thought, *he had a good feeling about this voyage and the next step in their fight against Camazotz.*

Epilogue

Half an hour later, Jack's stomach had settled and the friends decided to go down to their cabin. As he followed the other two to the stairway, Jack squinted up at the sails overhead. They had a following wind, and the crew had hoisted the sails to speed their progress. They shone in the moonlight against the dark night sky.

As Jack gazed upward, a black shape fluttered across one white sail—a bat! Jack froze, staring fixedly at it, wondering whether it could possibly be an ordinary, natural bat, and *not* Camazotz or one of his vampires. But it flew all around the ship in a horribly purposeful way. And it was very big.

Jack tapped Ben on the arm and pointed.

Ben and Emily both stopped and glanced up. Emily gasped, but Ben merely raised an eyebrow. "Well, he's not going to get an invitation to land like that, is he?" he remarked with a chuckle.

And sure enough, the bat continued to circle overhead, never settling—not even on a spar or a rope.

"Do you think it's Camazotz?" Emily asked.

"Yes," Ben replied with absolute certainty. "It's exactly the right size."

Jack couldn't take his eyes off the creature. He felt safer when he could see it.

"He can't fly forever," Ben said. "He'll have to go back to land eventually."

Sure enough, the bat finally wheeled away, its red eyes glowing angrily in the darkness. And the *Bernadette* sailed on into the night, carrying the friends ever closer to Mexico and to a new adventure in the Yucatán.

Don't miss the next installment in the

VAMPIRE PLAGUES TRILOGY

BOOK THREE
MEXICO

Here's an exclusive peek at the first chapter

The Gulf of Mexico stretched as far as the eye could see in every direction. The schooner *Providence* sped across the sea, her sails curved and taut in the wind. The ship's bow sliced cleanly through the waves with bursts of white spray. Perched at the top of the mainmast, Jack Harkett whooped with glee.

Jack had asked one of the sailors to show him how to climb the rigging almost as soon as the *Providence* had left New Orleans. He loved it up here.

They were already well into the second day of their journey and there was no land in sight. New Orleans was far behind them to the north, and the Yucatán peninsula — their destination in Mexico — lay ahead.

The Yucatán. Once the name had meant nothing to Jack. Now it meant danger and death and vampires. He knew the region was thick with dense jungle and scattered with ruins left by the ancient Mayan people. And he knew that a dark force had once ruled there — a god who demanded the blood of human sacrifice. A god whose bloodlust had weakened the once-powerful civilization, and ultimately destroyed the empire. The Mayans had vanished, their cities had crumbled, and the god, Camazotz, had fallen into forgotten legend. His name meant little to anyone nowadays, save in shadowy corners of Mexico where it was still whispered with fear.

Jack had come face-to-face with Camazotz and his vampire servants. Not in the depths of the Yucatán jungle but in London, and then again in Paris. Camazotz's plague of vampires had threatened both cities until the ancient god had been defeated by Jack and his friends Ben and Emily Cole.

In Paris they had learned that Camazotz was intent on finding and assembling the four pieces of an amulet that would give him power beyond imagining. He had already obtained three of those pieces. The friends had left France one step ahead of their enemy, armed with parchments that contained vital information about the amulet. They were determined to find the fourth and final piece before Camazotz could get ahold of it. But Camazotz needed those parchments, too, for they alone held the secret of where the fourth piece of the amulet could be found. Jack knew that the demon god would not be far behind them.

Jack glanced down from his perch and let his gaze sweep the deck. At the stern, he could see the *Providence*'s captain, Skip, at the wheel. He was tall and tanned from his many days at sea beneath the fierce southern sun.

As Jack watched, Emily Cole came out of the deckhouse and made her way forward to join her brother, Ben, who sat at the base of the bowsprit, a sort of third mast that stuck out straight ahead of the boat. Ben was gazing out to sea thoughtfully. He was twelve, the same age as Jack, and dressed similarly in a linen shirt and canvas trousers. Only Ben's fair hair set the two boys apart. Jack wondered how Ben felt about returning to the Yucatán. He had been there before, on a scientific expedition that had been destroyed by the newly awoken Camazotz. Ben had lost his father, Harrison; his godfather, Edwin Sherwood; and his family's oldest friend, Sir Donald Finlay, to Camazotz and his vampires. For Ben, the Yucatán held terrible memories.

Jack sighed and turned his attention to the distant horizon. The sun and the endless sky seemed to fill him with light and air and hope. And just then, he spotted something in the distance. "Hey, I can see land! There's land ahead!"

"Well, it wasn't entirely unexpected." Skip laughed as he leaned on the roof of the deckhouse with a telescope to his eye. Jack, Ben, and Emily gathered around, straining their unaided eyes to see if they could spot the land themselves. Down on the deck it wasn't so easy.

"We are on course, and I pride myself on being a halfway decent navigator," Skip added, lowering the telescope and winking at Jack. "Still 'n' all, you got good eyes, son."

Skip glanced at the sun. It was nearing the horizon. Jack

had learned to treat the sunset with great respect. Sunset was when the vampires came out. By day, they had to shelter undercover, or wrap up well against the sun's rays. But at night, they were free to roam at will. *The best thing about being in the middle of the ocean*, Jack thought, *was knowing that when the sun went down, the only thing he had to worry about was seeing in the dark.*

"We'll sail through the night. Should raise Puerto Morelos 'bout eight, nine o'clock in the morning if the wind holds." Skip folded up the telescope with a decisive snap, then something caught his eye. He opened the telescope again and peered into the distance. "Say, someone's in a hurry."

The friends craned their necks to see what they could. Against the dark blur of the Yucatán on the horizon, they could just make out a white speck, drawing closer. It was the sails of another boat.

"Big boat, three masts . . ." Skip murmured with the telescope to his eye. "And in a stiff breeze like this, he's got way too much sail on. Taller the mast is, the more it bends and the quicker it breaks, but some people just can't be told."

"He's coming straight at us," Ben said thoughtfully. The three friends exchanged glances, and Jack knew they were all thinking the same thing: *Could it be Camazotz?*

But Jack knew it was unlikely. Camazotz was behind them; this boat was coming from the Yucatán. And the sun was still shining brightly. It would be difficult for vampires to sail a boat under those conditions.

Skip patted Ben on the shoulder. "Don't worry, son. By

the time he gets here, assuming he holds that course, we'll be miles away. Sea's a big place, y'know."

Dinner was a stew of chopped chicken and sausage with onions and garlic. The cook was serving second helpings when Skip shouted, "Ready about!" from above.

The friends braced themselves. They knew Skip's command meant the ship was about to change direction. Still, it was an unusually sharp turn.

"Get the reefs out of the mainsail and break out the flying jib! Come on, move it!" Skip shouted from above. And they heard the sound of the crew running to obey their captain's orders, their footsteps echoing on the deck overhead.

"Now that don't sound good," the cook muttered. He quickly headed up on deck.

The friends looked at one another, and then they, too, headed for the stairs.

The ship they had seen earlier was much closer — no more than two hundred yards away now — and a bow wave of white water foamed before her. She was larger than the *Providence*, with three masts and square-rigged sails.

Ben's eyes fell to the men lining the rail nearest the *Providence*. He realized with a chill that several of them carried rifles and a few held crossbows. A man in the bow was shouting instructions in Spanish across the gap of water.

"What's he saying?" Ben asked Emily. Her Spanish was much better than his.

"He wants us to drop our sails and let him come aboard," Emily replied.

Skip was at the wheel, keeping one eye on the other ship and one eye on the thrumming mainsail above him.

"Who are these men?" Ben called to him.

Skip looked down and saw the three friends for the first time. "Now you three get below, y'hear?" he shouted anxiously.

"Are they pirates?" Emily asked nervously, not taking her gaze from the other vessel.

"Could be, ma'am, could be. Pirates used to be a frequent hazard in the Caribbean till your Royal Navy flushed 'em out. Never known 'em to come this far west, but there's a first time for everything. They don't mean us well, whoever they are."

"Can we outrun them?" Jack asked.

Skip snorted. "Little ship like us, son? Nuh-uh. We've only got two masts and two sails, while they can haul up more canvas just as they like. More canvas, more speed — that's how it goes. But we might be able to outmaneuver them. Ready about!"

He spun the wheel and the *Providence* turned her sharp prow into the wind. Overhead, the boom of the mainmast swung across the deck. The crew scrambled to haul in on the backstay, tightening the sail against the wind. Within a matter of seconds, the *Providence* was heading in a completely different direction, away from the stranger.

Ben glanced back at the other ship. She, too, was turning, but much more slowly. Her sailors were running around on deck, hauling in their own sails. Even from this distance, the crew didn't look as well organized as Skip's men.

"We're lighter, more maneuverable, and we can get much closer to the wind than they can," Skip said. "On the other hand, they're just plain faster than us, so it kind of evens out. Now I gave y'all an order to get below. You're underfoot and, besides, there might be fighting."

"We can fight!" Jack told him.

Skip smiled grimly. "Sure, son. I bet you're real handy with your fists, but these guys have guns. Now for the last time, get yourselves below, 'fore I have you carried down."

The three friends reluctantly ducked back down into the cabin. They tried to follow what was going on above by listening to the sounds from the deck. The *Providence* lurched again several times, zigzagging her way across the Gulf as Skip tried to shake off their pursuers.

Then all three friends jumped as they heard a muffled *boom*, followed immediately by the hiss and crack of something flying through the air not far overhead. Startled shouts echoed down from the deck above.

Ben stood on tiptoes to peer out of the skylight. He only caught a glimpse of the other boat, now very close indeed, but it was enough. He could see the cannon mounted on a swivel in the other ship's bow. "That was a warning shot!" he exclaimed. "They've got a cannon on deck. The *Providence* can't outrun a cannonball."

And sure enough, the *Providence* was slowing down. Up above, the crewmen were hauling in the sails. Within moments, the larger ship was drawing alongside. A shadow fell across the skylight and the cabin darkened as the other ship moved in.

Footsteps thumped on the deck above as men jumped aboard from the larger vessel. The friends looked at one another.

"It can't be Camazotz, can it?" Emily asked nervously.

"I really think it's only pirates," Ben said, and frustration welled up inside him. Had they really come this far, fought evil creatures from the depths of hell, and risked their lives only to be thwarted by a bunch of violent, greedy sea-thieves?

Up on deck, a harsh voice was shouting orders in Spanish. Then footsteps sounded on the stairs, and a man entered the cabin. He was dressed like a sailor, but he carried a pistol in one hand and some kind of spear in the other. He cast an eye over the three friends and shouted back up the stairs. Other men appeared behind him.

Ben frowned. "They look Mayan," he whispered, "not Mexican."

"*No mueva. Quede allá,*" the first man ordered.

"He said: 'Don't move. Stay where you are,'" Emily said quietly. One of the other men had pulled out his gun and was pointing it at them.

The first man moved past them to search the ship. He held the spear in front of himself defensively. Ben wondered why he chose to rely on the spear when he also carried a gun.

Once the man had satisfied himself that there was nobody else on board, he came back and looked thoughtfully at Ben, Emily, and Jack. Then he grasped his spear firmly in both hands and began to advance.

Ben and Jack immediately stepped in front of Emily. Ben was frantically casting his eyes around the cabin for something he could use as a weapon.

"Hold!" came a sharp command in English from the stairs. "Leave them be."

Ben turned his attention to the newcomer. Something about his voice was familiar.

The man with the spear stepped back obediently as the newcomer entered the cabin. Light from the skylight fell on his face, and Ben felt his jaw drop as he stared in shock and disbelief.

Standing in front of him, slightly thinner and grayer than Ben remembered, but nevertheless very much alive, was a man who Ben had been certain was dead. His father's best friend and his own godfather, the man who had sacrificed himself to Camazotz so that Harrison and Ben might escape the vampires. Edwin Sherwood now confronted his godson, with a loaded crossbow trained on Ben's heart.